"A gloriously sweet holiday read about expectations and reality."
—Kirkus Reviews

"A town called Christmas. An iffy wish come true. A new girl who could change it all. *All I Want For Christmas Is The Girl Next Door* kept me on my toes, turning pages from the start, and loving each revelation as it unfolded. Deep, funny, and real—this holiday romance will completely warm your heart and remind you that not all wishes should come true."
—Nova McBee, author of the *Calculated* Series

"Full of charm, wit, and so much warmth, Bobulski's *All I Want For Christmas Is The Girl Next Door* will have you breaking out in Christmas carols and will melt even the coldest heart!"
—Erin A. Craig, NYT Bestselling Author of *House of Salt and Sorrows*

"A cozy winter read you'll want to wrap yourself in like a blanket. At once bittersweet and hopeful, Bobulski thoughtfully explores the question of whether what we want is truly what we need against a backdrop of snowflakes, Christmas floats, and plenty of fresh cookies. A timeless holiday classic."
—Natalie Mae, author of *The Kinder Poison*

"This story is as magical as a shooting star on a cold winter night. Chelsea Bobulski's thoughtful and romantic exploration of true love and destiny will have readers swooning and wishing for her next Christmas novel!"
—Kristy Boyce, author of *Hot British Boyfriend*

"A fun frolic through the most wonderful time of the year! Full of heart and humor, this lighthearted twist on being careful what you wish for sparkles with delightful dialogue, swoony romance, and an ending that tugs at your heart before making it soar. Bobulski makes you think about being so focused on what we want that we miss what we already have. A holiday must-read!"
—Lori Goldstein, author of *Love, Theodosia, Sources Say,* and *Screen Queens*

"The charm of a small-town Hallmark Christmas meets the longing and wish fulfillment of John Green's Paper Towns in this magical holiday read. Expertly woven with strings of romance, ribbons of hope, and the sparkling power of gratitude, *All I Want For Christmas Is The Girl Next Door* is the perfect holiday story to curl up with on a snowy day. I adored every page!"
— Lorie Langdon, best-selling author of *Doon,* and *Olivia Twist*

"This is the book equivalent of drinking a mug of hot chocolate while listening to Christmas music as snowflakes gently fall outside. An all-around comforting, hopeful, and festive holiday read that will make you feel as cozy as your favorite Christmas movies."
—Kerry Winfrey, author of *Waiting for Tom Hanks*

# All I Want For Christmas is

## the girl in charge

## CHELSEA BOBULSKI

WISE WOLF BOOKS · LAS VEGAS

WISE WOLF
BOOKS

ALL I WANT FOR CHRISTMAS IS THE GIRL IN CHARGE

WISE WOLF BOOKS
An Imprint of Wolfpack Publishing

For information, address Wolfpack Publishing,
5130 S. Fort Apache Road, 215-380 Las Vegas, NV 89148
wisewolfbooks.com

Cover design by Wise Wolf Books

ISBN 978-1-953944-17-7 (paperback) 978-1-953944-55-9 (ebook)
LCCN: 2021945448

First Edition: November 2021

# All I Want For Christmas is

## the girl in charge

To Jane, who shares the same name as one of my favorite authors, and without whom Books 2-4 of this series would not exist. Thank you—for everything.

# 1

## Beckett

\*\*\*

The family in front of me looks happy. Two kids under four, with a third baby on the way. The husband wraps his arm around his wife, his hand cupping the swell of her belly, as if he can't stand to be more than a foot apart from her. She leans into him, nestling her head in the crook of his shoulder, while the kids chase each other around in circles at their feet. Sometimes she looks up at her husband and laughs; sometimes she breaks apart from him to ask the kids if they prefer this tree to the one they saw before, reminding them to watch out for the saw I hold at my side, but she always goes back to her husband, slipping into the crook of his shoulder and wrapping her arm around his back.

They're exactly the kind of family I used to wonder what it would be like to have. Parents who loved each other. Siblings. Maybe a dog. I'd bet money this family has a golden retriever waiting for them back home. But I don't wonder what it would be like to live in the same place long enough to grow roots anymore, being part of a family that radiates warmth and comfort and belonging. Having the kind of childhood where I would have never heard the words *rehab* and *children's services* and *foster families*.

Wondering has never made anything better.

So I ignore their happiness, even though I know the polite thing to do would be to smile back at them and nod my head and act like I care about finding them the perfect Christmas tree. And if I feel any jolt of pain at their happiness, it's soft. A distant echo of a grief I buried long ago.

"Can we get this one, Daddy? Can we, can we, pleeeeease?" The little girl asks, jumping up and down next to a blue spruce while her little brother weaves in and out of the trees with his arms stretched out, making airplane noises.

Her dad laughs and glances at me. "Looks like we've found our tree."

"Yay!" The little girl shouts, then promptly falls into the white powder at her feet and starts making snow angels. Her brother follows suit, plopping down into the snow with a giggle.

Their mom's eyes twinkle as she meets my gaze. "We just love this time of year. You must love it too, working at a Christmas tree farm."

I shrug. "It's my uncle's."

The woman frowns slightly. Over her shoulder, I see Aunt Bee standing ten feet away, gesturing for me to smile. I force my mouth to twitch upward. It feels unnatural, like someone put a fishing hook on either side of my lips and pulled.

"I'll cut it down and tie it to your car while my uncle rings you up," I tell them.

The couple still looks uncertain of me—maybe it's the tendrils of a tattoo snaking out of the hem of my sleeve or the barbell spiking through the cartilage of my left ear—but they're trying hard not to show it.

Behind them, Aunt Bee makes a "keep talking" gesture, so I add, "There's free hot cocoa in the gift shop too. If you want some."

"Thank you," the mom says, pulling away from her husband to help the kids up. "Did you hear that, guys? Hot cocoa!"

They scream and race for the red barn that holds the gift shop on this side of the property, a smaller replica of the barn next to Uncle Bill's farmhouse across the street, where he stores all of his farming equipment and machinery. I missed the summer harvest in the north field, but I got here in time to help set up the haunted corn maze that ran through October. Not that I was dying to be out on a harvester in the summer heat, but the hours would've been good.

That's the unit of time I think in these days. Not days. Not weeks. Not months.

Hours.

Aunt Bee starts walking toward me, but she's stopped by an older couple who apparently know her, not that that's a surprise in a town as small as Christmas, Virginia. I bend down, place the saw against the base of the trunk, and cut into the pulp.

This is my favorite part of the job. Nobody talks to the guy with the saw. I can just focus on the slicing of the serrated blade; on the snap and release as the tree pitches forward; on the weight of the branches as I place the tree on a sled and haul it to the parking lot; on the wrapping of the twine around the roof of the car and the knots that Uncle Bill, an OG Eagle Scout, taught me how to do when I first arrived. I'm thankful that this time is no exception—Aunt Bee doesn't get away from the couple until I've already secured the tree to the top of the family's car and watched them drive away.

She comes to a stop next to me, waving at the kids, who grin at us through the rear windshield as their car pulls onto the interstate.

"You need to smile more," she tells me, barely moving her lips through her own cemented grin as she continues waving.

"People come here for a tree. I give them a tree," I reply.

The car disappears around a curve.

Aunt Bee turns to me. "They don't just come here for a tree. They come here for an experience. Some of them drive hours from home specifically to come *here*, where they know they'll get the kind of holiday cheer that memories are made of. It ruins the magic if you don't smile."

I try to care—really, I do—but I just can't find anything inside of me that hasn't frozen over, solid as the ground beneath my feet. So I nod, once, and hope that's enough.

She stares at me a moment longer before nudging my ribs. "Come on. I've got an errand to run."

"I was planning on working until dinner."

"It won't take long. An hour or two, tops."

I grit my teeth. An hour or two with Aunt Bee always turns into three or four. She doesn't mean for it to, but she gets stopped everywhere she goes. Someone always seems to have something to say to her—some question they want to ask, an opinion they'd like for her to give. And okay, sure, to most people, a couple hours isn't that big of a deal, but to me, it's everything. I'm already having a hard enough time finding hours for the farm as it is, between school and homework (homework I wouldn't even bother to do if my deal with the judge didn't include maintaining a 3.5 GPA).

I've been here for a month, and I've only managed eighteen of my required community service hours. Eighty-two to go.

"Come on, Aunt Bee," I say, lowering my voice so the other families won't hear. "You know I need the hours."

She considers this.

"Nope, sorry. I need big, strapping muscles to help me lug this trunk to the high school."

"Can't Uncle Bill do it?"

"I said *strapping*."

"I heard that," Uncle Bill mutters from the outdoor cash register.

"You okay if I steal him for an hour, Bill?" Aunt Bee asks him.

"Reckon so."

"There," she says, clasping her hands together. "It's settled."

We cross the country road, our boots crunching snow-dusted gravel, then the asphalt of the highway, then gravel again as we start up the drive to the house. The trunk is sitting on the front porch, a beaten-up rectangle with strips of leather peeling off the corners and dark spots tarnishing the hardware.

"Managed to push it this far down from the attic, but I'll need you to get it the rest of the way."

I pick it up easily. It's not heavy, but it is awkward. I can see why Aunt Bee couldn't manage it on her own.

"What's in here?" I ask, following her to the car.

"Just some old stuff from the attic. The school's putting on *Pride and Prejudice* for their Christmas play, and Evelyn Waverley's been asking all of us older folks to help with the costumes and set pieces."

It doesn't surprise me to hear Evelyn's involved. You don't have to live in this town long to discover that if there's a charity drive, club meeting, or some other event going on, you'll find Evelyn Waverley at the center of it. She was even the first Christmas High student I met. As senior class president, she'd volunteered to show me around my first day.

I can still see her standing in front of the school, talking to some guy I later found out was Kyle Caldwell, Christmas High's star running back. It was obvious to everyone that he was flirting with her, but Evelyn was too focused on answering some question he'd asked about their Pre-Calc homework to notice.

I'm not sure why I zeroed in on her. There were at least fifty other students hanging out in the courtyard that morning. A Frisbee flew overhead, and some guys chased after it, elbowing one another to get to it, while another group stood in a circle, a Hacky Sack bouncing back and forth off their shoes and kneecaps. People hugged and high-fived and commiserated over an upcoming test. School buses came and went. It was loud and crowded and chaotic. There was no reason she should have noticed me while I was still a good fifteen feet away from her, and I guess, looking back, there was no reason for me to notice her either. I didn't know she'd volunteered to show me around, and yet, somehow, my eyes locked onto her the second I stepped onto the school's brick pathway.

I remember watching her easygoing smile and the tiny dimple it cast in her cheek; remember noticing the way the early morning sun shone like gold against her honey-colored hair; remember her turning away from Kyle, her eyes, the color of bottle glass washed smooth by the sea, finding me in the crowd. And then that smile that had been meant for Kyle widened and became mine, and even though if anyone had asked me, I would've told them I was far past feeling anything these days, my breath caught at the sight of her.

"Beckett?" she'd asked, her voice clear and resonant, like the sound a pure crystal goblet makes when someone runs a dampened finger over the rim. "Beckett Hawthorne?"

I'd frowned, not sure why she should know my name. "Yeah?"

"I'm Evelyn Waverley." She held out her hand. "I volunteered to show you around. Ready to get started?"

In that moment I knew I would've followed her any-where, and that revelation unsettled me. No one should have that much power over any one person. Especially not over someone they just met.

I've avoided her since that day. Well, as much as I can. She has her hand in everything. Student council, the school paper, three different clubs—not that I belong to any of them—and now, apparently, the school play.

I tell myself that I'm not really avoiding her. We only have one class together (AP English with Mrs. Warren, because my social worker refused to let me skate by with just art classes and study halls), and if I walk the other way when I see her coming, I tell myself it's because I forgot which way I was supposed to be going or because I'm not interested in getting roped into whatever project she's currently heading—not because I don't want to risk feeling that same earth-shattering, everything-changing, unexplainable magnetic *pulse* that echoed in my soul the moment her eyes met mine.

I try to make it sound like I'm just making conversation as I ask, "Evelyn's in the play?"

Aunt Bee nods. "Playing Elizabeth Bennet, I believe. That's one of my favorite books, you know. Bill gave it to me our first Christmas together. We were fourteen."

"Is that why it's one of your favorites?" I ask. "Because Bill gave it to you?"

She waves off my question. "Him giving it to me has noth-ing to do with it being a good book."

I don't reply as she opens the door to the backseat of her car, and I slide the trunk in. I'm not sure what the deal is with Aunt Bee and Uncle Bill (technically, my Great Aunt Bee and Great Uncle Bill, which I think can be confusing for people in a town where literally *everyone* calls her Aunt Bee). I'd only met them a couple times throughout my childhood, and they weren't married for any of it. They co-own both of their businesses, the farm and the bookstore, along with the house, even though Aunt Bee rents an apartment above her store. Every time I saw them before now, they would alternate between laughing like the best of friends and bickering like the oldest married couple, and even though I never once saw Bill put his arm around Bee, they were like the husband and wife who'd just left the lot—always circling each other, never more than a dozen feet away, like there was a gravitational pull between them whenever they were together, never allowing them to get too far apart. And now that I'm living with Bill, Aunt Bee comes over at least once a day to check on me and see how business is going. Maybe she did that before I arrived, or maybe it's a new thing. Either way, for two people who've been divorced since before I was born, they sure do spend a lot of time together.

I close the door and rap my knuckles on the roof. "You can take it from here, can't you?"

She grins at me. "Nice try. In the car, mister."

I sigh. "Yes, ma'am."

My stomach does a little flip as I slide into the passenger seat, but not in a good way.

Seeing Evelyn Waverley is the last thing I want to do.

# 2

## *Evelyn*

### ✳✳✳

I'm pretty sure I've been in love with Mr. Darcy since I was ten years old, when my Aunt Allison gave me her crinkled, dog-eared copy of *Pride and Prejudice*. It was the last day of school before Christmas break, and I'd run home crying because Dennis Reedy had called me an "ugly brownnosing teacher's pet" in front of our entire fifth grade class after my science fair project beat his for first place. His friends had joined in next, saying it was no wonder nobody liked me.

No one disagreed. A few others even nodded.

I was devastated.

My aunt, who had been getting her PhD in British literature at Oxford at the time, had flown home a week early for Christmas, and she was sitting at our kitchen counter, working on her thesis, her fingers clacking away on her laptop, when I ran in. Mom and Dad were still at work, and at first, I didn't want to tell her what was wrong, but then she offered to make me hot cocoa, and it all spilled out while she warmed a pot of milk on the stove.

I waited for her to tell me all of the usual things—that he was jealous, and I should just ignore him, that I shouldn't apologize for working hard or for winning—but instead, she sat me down, looked me square in the eyes, and said, "I hate to break it you, kid, but there are going to be a lot of Dennis Reedys in your life. It comes with the territory when you're ambitious and work hard for what you want."

"I know, I know." I'd heard all of this before. "I just need to learn how to ignore him."

"No, sweets. Ignoring him is the absolute worst thing you could do."

My brow furrowed. That was *so* not the advice I'd gotten from countless Mom and Dad lectures.

Allison sighed at my confusion, turned off the stove, grabbed two coffee mugs from the cupboard, and poured the hot chocolate. Then, taking my hand, she said, "Come here. I want to show you something."

She led me to the half bath in the hall and pointed to the mirror.

"Tell me what you see."

I shrugged and looked down at the floor. All I saw was a girl with red eyes and tear-stained cheeks that nobody liked.

Allison cupped her hand under my chin and tilted my face up, into the light. "I see a girl who knows what she wants and isn't afraid to work hard for it. I see a girl who is fierce and strong and so far above every Dennis Reedy in the world that all they're ever going to want to do is bring her down to their level and make her feel worthless in the process. But you're not going to let them do it, because you know your worth. You know there is a world-changer inside of you racing to get out. You feel it, don't you? That surge of energy, like there's something inside of you that's always trying to run ahead of everyone else, something you can't contain? That's passion, baby girl. That's ambition. That's *wildfire*, and not a single person in this world can snuff it out without your permission. So the next time a Dennis Reedy says something awful to you, let it feed the flames. Instead of letting it bring you down, let it push you forward. Don't ignore it. *Use it.* Understand?"

I ran my hands under my eyes and nodded.

"Good."

She led me back into the kitchen, handing me my mug. Then she crossed to the chair she'd been sitting in, reached into the satchel she'd slung across the back, and pulled out a book.

"And when good people are hard to come by," she'd said, holding it out to me, "we find them in books, and in the authors who had the good sense to write them."

I'd refused, at first, to take the book from her. It was clear from the bent spine and underlined pages that it was well loved, but Allison just shook her head, saying she'd been meaning to get a new copy for years, and this gave her the perfect excuse.

I started reading it that night. It was hard to get used to the language at first, and I used a dictionary app on my phone for all of the words I didn't understand, but somewhere along the way I found comfort in the language, in the cadence and rhythm of it, and in the way everyone seemed to have a large-enough vocabulary to explain every possible feeling a human being could hold inside of themselves.

And, of course, I fell in love with Darcy, with the goodness in him underneath the proud exterior, but not just him. I fell in love with Elizabeth and her ability to speak her mind without fear; with Jane and her kindness toward everyone; with Mr. Bingley and his cheerfulness; even with Mr. Bennet, who seemed well ahead of his time in the ways he encouraged Elizabeth to be herself and not apologize for it. And, in falling in love with the characters, I fell in love with the author, with this woman who could write other strong women in a time that isn't really known for its feminist ideals.

I quickly read every other Jane Austen novel and transformed my room to fit my new obsession, with framed, vintage artwork featuring men and women in Regency clothing; posters from every single Jane Austen movie; and even a picture of Jane Austen herself. I'd added other female writers too, to both my bookshelves and my walls—Edith Wharton and Mary Shelley and Shirley Jackson and George Eliot and Elizabeth Goudge—but Austen remained my favorite, and Allison's copy of *Pride and Prejudice* was now even more tattered and dog-eared than it was when she first gave it to me. When it wasn't in my backpack or in my purse, it sat on my bedside table, ready for whenever I needed to find the same comfort I'd found in its pages during that first reading.

So it was really no wonder that when I met with my guidance counselor last May to go over the list of colleges I'd be applying to this fall, and he told me I would need to do something big to get the Ivy League to notice me, I found the solution in the book that always seemed to hold all of the answers. I told Mrs. Warren, the theater director and senior English teacher, my plan. She signed off on it, and I immediately got to work, writing my very own stage adaptation of *P&P*. It took me all summer and most of September too, but with Mrs. Warren's guidance, we ended up with a ninety-minute play: *A Pride and Prejudice Christmas*.

I just knew, deep down in my bones, that a girl who had written, co-directed, and starred in her very own Jane Austen adaptation had to be worth a second look from any admission office in the world.

And now, three weeks from opening night, everything I've worked so hard for is slipping through my fingers, all

because Greg Bailey, the boy who is *supposed* to be playing
Mr. Darcy, decided to make a video of himself dancing his
way to Thanksgiving dinner, tripped over the Duplo village
his twin brothers had left at the top of the staircase, and
broke his leg in three places.

In short, it's very possible that the next time I see Greg
Bailey, I'm going to kill him.

My phone keeps *bing*-ing as two of my best friends—Isla
Riddle and Savannah Mason—text back and forth in our
group chain. Isla keeps repeating what a disaster this is, and
Savannah's repeatedly threatening to break Greg's other leg,
even though I told her that would only help a little bit.

*Bing.*

*Bing.*

*BING.*

My head is pounding, and my chest is tightening and
I'm pretty sure I'm nanoseconds away from diving headfirst
into a full-blown panic attack as I pull my powder-blue 1966
Volkswagen Beetle into the nearly empty school parking lot
and take a spot right across from the auditorium. My phone
rings as I put my car in park and grab the coffee I picked up
from the bakery on the way here. I check the caller ID.

Mrs. Warren.

I step out of the car and answer the phone. "Hello?"

"Evelyn? Where are you? I'm hyperventilating."

"I'm walking up now," I tell her, swinging my bubble-
gum-pink backpack over my shoulder and crossing the courtyard to the auditorium's side entrance. "Be there in a sec."

The thing I love most about Mrs. Warren is that she takes
everything just as seriously as I do, which makes us a great
team when it comes to getting things done but also kind of
backfires when we have a situation on our hands. I never
thought I'd be considered the calm, collected one—especially when we don't have a chance in Santa's sweatshop of

finding a replacement good enough to keep the production going—but here we are. We've only managed to convince two guys from the entire student body to try out today, one of whom is only doing so because he talked back to Mrs. Warren in class and chose this over detention.

I text *NOT HELPING* to my friends in huge letters, followed by three hand-slapping-face emojis, as I walk, the barely-there tread on my ankle boots crunching blue salt cubes on the shoveled walkway.

**Savannah:** *Sorry, but I could just kill him.*

**Isla:** *Get in line, sister.*

I send back a frustrated emoji before silencing my phone and stuffing it into my back pocket.

The handle of the backstage door feels like ice in my hand as I swing it open, and then I'm breathing in the comforting smell of old plank floors, hot stage lights, and velvet-cushioned chairs. Mrs. Warren's tiny office sits off to the side of the door, and old set pieces gather dust behind the stage's one and only curtain. I kick off my wet-from-the-snow boots so I don't track anything onstage, drop my backpack and coffee onto Mrs. Warren's desk, then jog into the main part of the auditorium.

Mrs. Warren's sitting in the front row with her head in her hands, the rest of the cast and crew looking just as worried behind her. No one seems to have started doing anything yet, and, for just a split second, I hesitate, knowing it won't do my control-freak reputation any favors to take charge, but then my aunt's voice ricochets through my head—*"I see a girl who knows what she wants and isn't afraid to work hard for it"*—and I clap my hands together, getting everyone's attention.

"All right, guys. I know things look bleak, but this show is getting canceled over my dead body, so let's get to work. Jen," I say, hurrying off the stage, the old, wooden stairs creaking beneath me, "take Cody and work on memorizing lines. Start with the Meryton assembly, where Jane and Mr. Bingley first meet."

Jen nods and takes Cody's hand, pulling him toward the corner of the room. His cheeks turn pink, and he can't stop staring at her fingers intertwined with his. I want to tell him to ask her out already, but the last thing we need is for our Mr. Bingley to pass out from sheer embarrassment and crack his head open on the linoleum, so I just shake my head at them and turn toward the front row, where arguably the cutest couple in Christmas High history is currently sitting.

"Graham, Piper," I say, getting their attention. "We still need design sketches for the last six scenes."

"On it," Graham replies, putting one arm around Piper's chair and pulling a notepad out of his backpack with the other. They were put in charge of set design for the spring musical last year after everyone saw how amazing their float was for the Christmas parade, and I just know they're going to crush this play too.

Assuming there even *is* a play.

I rub my chest right beneath my collarbone, where it feels like someone has wrapped a rope around my ribs. I push the feeling aside. *Focus. You will figure this out.*

I turn to Sarah Clarke next, who's sitting on her boyfriend Jeremy's lap, sharing a bag of Cheetos and a Coke.

"Sarah, take the dance troupe and teach them that choreography you showed me for the Netherfield ball. And, Jeremy, I want to go over some ideas for lighting and sound in a minute, so have your script out and ready."

Jeremy salutes me. "You got it, boss."

Sarah licks Cheeto dust off her delicate, ballerina fingers and pushes out of his lap. "Do you really think we're going to be able to find someone to take Greg's place?"

"I'll find someone, even if I have to recruit him from

another district."

I sound intense even to my own ears, but I can't help it. Everything I've worked so hard for, all of the hours I've spent writing and agonizing over the script, all of the lines I've already memorized and the casting we've already done and the set pieces that have already been painted, could now, because of one person, go up in smoke.

*Why* didn't I cast an understudy?

Oh, yeah. Because not enough guys auditioned.

Sometimes going to a small school *really* sucks.

"Where are the boys who are supposed to be trying out?" I ask Mrs. Warren, my chest even tighter than before, like I'm halfway up the incline of a giant roller coaster—heart pounding, adrenaline rushing, my mind already anticipating the way my stomach is going to drop when we crest the top of the hill. As long as I don't give in, I'll be okay, but if I go over that edge, there'll be no stopping the panic attack once it starts.

Mrs. Warren doesn't look up, just waves vaguely behind her. I glance at the back of the auditorium, where Luke Fisher—the boy who chose this over detention—twiddles his thumbs on his phone, earbuds blocking out the rest of the world, and another boy—who must be a freshman even though he looks like he's twelve—stands next to a woman who could only be his mom, fiddling with the cuffs of his sweater.

I start up the aisle, coming to a stop in front of the freshman. I don't feel like dealing with Luke's attitude right off the bat, and who knows? Maybe this kid will surprise me and be so good we won't even need Luke to try out. It's wishful thinking, judging from the fact that he already looks like he's going to puke, but it's worth a try.

"Is he okay?" I ask his mom as sweat drips from his forehead.

"He's fine," his mom replies. "Just a little stage fright."

If that's a little, I'd hate to see a lot.

"What's your name?" I ask him.

"Stephen McElhenny," his mom says, stepping in front of him. She bends closer to my ear and lowers her voice. "I'm not expecting him to get the role, but he really needs to get over this fear of crowds. He'll never be able to do anything with his life if he doesn't."

My brow furrows. "I'm not sure that's true—"

"Stephen, you're up, honey," his mom says, ignoring me. "Here, I'll take your jacket."

It takes a few tugs, but his mom finally rips the jacket out of his white-knuckled fingers.

"All right." I look up and down his shivering, five-foot-four frame. "Let's see what you've got."

His face turns a darker shade of green.

I put my arm around his shoulders, leading him down the aisle, away from his mom. "It's okay. It's just me and Mrs. Warren watching you. Everyone else is busy doing their own thing. Take a deep breath. That's it. In and out. Better?"

He nods, dabbing his sleeve across his glistening forehead. "I really hate public speaking. I'm only doing it because my mom is making me."

"I kind of got that. Just try to have fun, okay? We're not going to make you do anything you don't want to do. Just give us your best shot, and then get out of here. Sound good?"

He lets out a shaky breath. "Yeah, okay. Thanks."

"No problem."

The side of me that loves productivity is screaming that this is a total waste of time, but I try to push that particular compulsion aside. There are some things that are more important than being productive (or so my mom tells me), and helping this kid out feels like the right thing to do, even if we won't be any closer to finding our Mr. Darcy at the end of it.

I hand him his script and tell him to read from the Meryton assembly scene, when Mr. Bingley suggests that Mr. Darcy should ask Elizabeth Bennet to be his dance partner, and Mr. Darcy responds with, "She is tolerable, but not handsome enough to tempt *me*." Cody's busy practicing with Jen, so I read Bingley's lines back to Stephen. The kid's voice is scratchy and goes up an octave every third word.

I can see why he didn't want to get up and speak in front of a bunch of people.

"You're doing great," I reassure him, holding up two fingers to indicate he only has two more lines to go.

He rushes through the last lines, then breathes a sigh of relief when he's done.

"Excellent," I tell him, winking. "We'll let you know if you got the part."

He hops off the stage like he can't get out of here fast enough.

"That was wonderful, darling, really wonderful," his mom tells him, putting his coat back around his shoulders as they head up the aisle.

Mrs. Warren still has her head in her hands.

"Luke," I bark. "You're next."

He doesn't look up from his phone.

"You've got to be kidding me," I grumble, marching back up the aisle. I rip out one of his earbuds. "Let's go."

He sighs and puts his phone away. "This is stupid."

"Would you rather have four weeks of detention instead? Because I heard that's what's on the table if you don't take this audition seriously."

"Hey, all Mrs. Warren told me was that I had to audition," he says, shoving his hands in his front hoodie pocket. "*Not* that I had to take it seriously."

"Well, I'm the co-director, and I'm telling you to take it seriously, or I'll make her give you six weeks instead."

He narrows his eyes at me like six weeks of detention might be worth it if it means he doesn't have to talk to me anymore.

I get that look more often than I would like.

"Fine," he bites back. "Give me the script."

I hand it over just as the theater doors open and Aunt Bee walks in carrying a to-go coffee from the bakery. Someone walks in behind her carrying a huge, old-fashioned trunk, but his upper torso is still in the shadows of the front entrance, and I can't tell who it is.

"Hey, Aunt Bee," I say, trying to leave my frustration toward Luke out of my voice. "Did you bring the antiques?"

"In the trunk," she replies, putting her arm around me and pulling me into a side hug. "How you doin', sugar?"

"I've been better. Greg Bailey broke his leg, and now we need to find a new Darcy or the play's going to be canceled."

"I heard. Any luck finding a replacement?"

I side-eye Luke, who already has his phone back out. "Not yet."

"*Hmm.*"

Aunt Bee is one of those people who can put a lot of meaning into a single "hmm", but before I can ask her what plot is brewing in her brain now, a familiar voice asks, "Where do you want this?"

I notice the tattoo first—the edges of sheet music slashing across his wrist—then the shaved sides of his head and the mop of dark hair on top, with its longer pieces that always fall into his eyes, and the silver arrow slicing across the ridge of his left ear, flashing gold in the light of the antique wall sconces.

Beckett. Hawthorne.

The first time I met him, everything around me—the conversations and the music and the cars driving by—muffled as if I had suddenly been plunged underwater. His dark hair fell into his eyes, just as it's doing now, and he pushed it back with his hand, something I've since learned he does often, usually when he's feeling nervous or uncomfortable. That was the first time I noticed the tattoo and the hardened callouses on his fingertips, although I couldn't begin to imagine what they were from. But it was his eyes—dark around the edges, with a starburst of caramel in the middle, ringed by lashes any girl would kill to have—that I couldn't look away from. He'd narrowed them at me slightly as I stared openmouthed at him, like he couldn't quite figure out what to make of me.

He'd seemed surprised that I knew immediately who he was, but it couldn't have taken him more than a day to figure out why. Christmas High is a small school, and we rarely get new kids. But there's a part of me that thinks, even if we went to one of those huge schools with two thousand students that you hear about in big cities, I would've noticed Beckett Hawthorne right away. Maybe it was in the way he looked at me, like he could somehow see down to the very core of me; or maybe it was in the way his voice thrummed in my ears, low and rumbling; or maybe it was in the way he carried himself, as if his skin were made of armor, hiding all of the vulnerable pieces of him somewhere far, far beneath.

But whatever attraction I felt toward him dissolved as soon as I got to know him.

I gave him the benefit of the doubt at first, thinking maybe he was shy because he never talked to anyone, never raised his hand in English, and whenever he *was* forced to speak, he answered with a yes or a no, even if Mrs. Warren asked him to elaborate, as if he only had so many words allotted to him in a day and couldn't be bothered to waste any of them on us. But then there was that day—my entire body cringes just thinking about it—when I was walking around a corner and overheard my name in a conversation between Beckett and Kyle Caldwell. I have no idea what started it or why Kyle would ask Beckett anything, let alone ask him about *me*, but I heard Kyle say, "So you're not interested in Evelyn, then?" And Beckett replied, "Why would I be?" and even though I didn't give two figgy puddings what Beckett Hawthorne thought, something about the way he said it, like I was the last person on earth he would *ever* consider as a romantic possibility, crushed me.

I've hated him on principle ever since.

I throw a forced smile at him for Aunt Bee's sake. "You can put it backstage."

Beckett doesn't even acknowledge that I've spoken. Just picks up the trunk and heads for the stairs.

I roll my eyes.

"Don't worry, dear," Aunt Bee says, misinterpreting my annoyance. "I'm sure the course will correct itself. It always does."

"Thanks, Aunt Bee."

She glances at Mrs. Warren over my shoulder. "Oh my, she seems a little down. I'm going to see if I can cheer her up."

I watch her walk down the aisle toward Mrs. Warren, taking the seat next to her, then I turn back to Luke and rip his earbud out again.

"Come on. Let's see what you've got."

He glares at me, stuffs his free hand in his pocket, and curls the script in his other hand.

"Page thirty," I tell him, directing him to the same scene I asked Stephen to perform. "From the top."

He gives me a serious scowl and, just for a moment, I let myself hope that maybe this attitude is *exactly* what we need from our Mr. Darcy. I straighten up a little, expecting his frustration to seep into the lines and give off the exact impression I'm going for, but he reads the lines like a robot—all monotone, no inflection, and much too slow, like he's *trying* to get on my every last nerve.

He finishes the scene and curls the script back up in his hand. "Are we done now?"

"Again. From the top."

He rolls his eyes. "Come on. There's no way you want to hear *that* again."

"I'm sorry, did I say you'd get six weeks of detention? I meant ten."

"You can't do that. You don't have that kind of power."

"Try me."

He exhales and takes a step forward, lowering his voice. "Look, Waverley, even if I give this audition my absolute best, which I'm not going to do, I still wouldn't be in your stupid play, so would you do us both a favor and *leave me alone?*"

I narrow my eyes at him. "Fine, but your mom's going to hear about this at our next festival committee meeting."

He scoffs. "Yeah, whatever."

"And your fly's down."

He scoffs again, then looks down and grumbles under his breath, pulling his zipper back up and walking offstage.

I take a seat in the front row and drop my head into my hands. A low chuckle rumbles behind me. I glance over my shoulder. Beckett's sitting in the next row back, his lips turned up in a half smirk.

"Can I help you with something?" I ask him.

"Nope," he says. "Just waiting for Aunt Bee."

"Well, wait a little quieter, would you?"

"I don't know what you're talking about. I'm just sitting here."

I glare at him.

He smirks back.

I'm about to tell him *exactly* where he can shove that smirk, but then an idea explodes in my brain like a firecracker. Forgetting Beckett completely, I shoot up out of my chair and yell, "Jeremy! Graham!"

Graham looks up from his notebook, where he and Piper have been sketching their latest ideas. Jeremy pops his head out of the sound booth.

"Yeah?" They both ask at the same time.

"Get over here and audition. One of you is going to be our Mr. Darcy."

"Umm," Graham says, "I don't think that's a good idea."

I cross my arms. "Don't tell me you have stage fright?"

"I mean, yeah, a little," Graham admits. "But I'm also just terrible. I don't act, and I'm not a great dancer, so it's probably best if I just save us all some time, sit back down in my comfortable seat, and focus on something I'm actually semi-good at."

"Ditto," Jeremy calls out.

I narrow my eyes at Graham. "I don't believe you."

"Piper back me up," Graham says, turning toward his girlfriend. "Tell her how awful I am."

Piper tucks a pencil behind her ear. "His dancing's actually much better than it used to be..."

All of the color drains from Graham's face. "What are you doing?"

"But no," she continues, giggling. "He's not ready for the stage."

"Fine." I turn toward Sarah, who's teaching the troupe the first steps of the Netherfield dance. "What about Jeremy?"

"Tell her how much I suck, honey," Jeremy yells across the auditorium. "Hold nothing back."

Sarah looks like she's trying to think of a nice way to agree with him. "He's...musically disinclined."

"HA! See?" Jeremy shouts. "I suck. Now let me go back to the shadows where my 'musically disinclined' self belongs."

"Darcy only dances once, you know," I inform them.

"Yeah, but it's kind of a big scene, right?" Graham points out. "I mean, it's where he starts to fall in love with Elizabeth, and I *definitely* cannot give off any kind of 'love vibes' if I'm tripping all over myself."

"It's true," Piper agrees. "He's really terrible at that."

"Thank you," Graham replies. "Wait, what?"

Piper grins at him.

I push the pads of my fingers into my eyes. "I don't think you guys realize that if we don't find our Mr. Darcy, we're screwed. We can't have a play without one of the main characters."

"We could always change the play," Sarah suggests. "Maybe do something a little less iconic?"

I shake my head. "We've already put too much time into this. We'd have to find a script that would work, recast the whole thing, go back to the drawing board for all of the set design, and completely forget all of the lines we've already memorized." Not to mention all of the hours I spent adapting the book. Besides, co-directing some random high school play won't make me look any different from any other teen applying to the Ivy League. "Our school has done countless run-of-the-mill plays, but we've never done *Pride and Prejudice*."

"Yeah, and I'm starting to see why," Jeremy shouts from the sound booth.

I grit my teeth. "Hey, Jer, if you don't want me to take you seriously as an actor, maybe don't show me how well you can project, okay?"

He gives me a thumbs-up and ducks back inside the booth.

And then I hear it, the low rumble of Beckett Hawthorne laughing again, and maybe it's because I haven't heard him laugh once in the month since he moved here but have now heard him laugh twice—both times at *me*—or maybe it's because I don't have an ounce of patience left, but whatever it is, something inside me *snaps*.

"You think this is funny?" I ask, whirling on him.

He covers his mouth with his hand, and I hate that I notice how toned the muscles in his forearm are beneath the pushed-up wrist of his flannel shirt.

"No," he says. "Of course not."

"No, seriously. Does my frustration amuse you?"

He bends forward, his elbows on his knees as he looks down at the ground, hiding his face, but I can still see his shoulders rising and falling with each burst of barely controlled laughter.

"If you think it's so easy," I tell him, "why don't you get up here and try it?"

He shakes his head. "I'm good."

"No, really," I say, crossing the stage so I'm standing right in front of him. "Here's the script."

"No, really," he repeats, leaning back in his seat. "I'm good."

"Oh, I get it. You know you'd be just as terrible as everyone else, so you'd rather laugh at those of us who are willing to try than put your own easily damaged ego on the line."

A challenge sparks in his eyes, but before he can respond, the front door creaks open and in walks—

Kyle Caldwell.

Everyone turns to him.

Kyle hesitates. "Sorry. Is it too late to audition?"

"You want to be in the play?" I ask, flabbergasted. He's wearing his crimson-and-evergreen letterman's jacket, along with last year's State Championship ring and the kind of sweatpants that look like they cost a hundred dollars.

"Yeah, well," he says, shifting slightly under the gaze of the entire cast, "I heard you were in a bind, and after State next week, my schedule is clear, so I thought...maybe..."

"Yes," I say quickly, before he can change his mind. "You can audition. Come on up."

Kyle smiles and jogs forward. I take my gaze off him for just a second, glancing at Beckett with a "Who's laughing now?" gleam in my eyes.

A muscle in Beckett's jaw ticks.

I hand Kyle the script and direct him to the same Meryton assembly scene as he heads onstage. I'm looking to see if he can exude that perfect balance of mystery and impoliteness. Basically, I need him to be a misunderstood jerk that the audience can still relate to and still want Elizabeth to fall in love with. Not an easy feat, and Kyle reads the lines a little flat for my taste, but his projection is good, and I can work with him on some of the inflections—give him direction as to how opinionated and proud Mr. Darcy is supposed to be at first before he starts to shed his icy exterior.

In short, he's the best one to audition yet, and I don't have time to be picky.

Kyle finishes and exhales loudly. "Man, that's more terrifying than running into a linebacker."

Everyone laughs.

"That was great, Kyle," I tell him, climbing the stairs and taking the rolled-up script back from him, smoothing it out with my hands (seriously, why does *everyone* roll it up?). "Really great. I think it's safe to say you've got the part."

"Wait."

Beckett stands and slides out of the second row, jumping up the stairs two at a time. He comes to a stop in front of me, his dark eyes boring into mine.

"Script," he says.

"Excuse me?"

"Script," he repeats through gritted teeth.

Of course. He's baiting me.

Well, two can play that game.

I shove the script into his chest, then turn to head back down the stairs. "Page twelve, the Meryton assembly scene—"

He grabs my hand, stopping me. "Oh no. If I'm doing this, you're doing it too. Pick a scene you're in."

I glance down at his fingers, so shocked at the feeling of his skin against mine that it takes me a second longer than it should to wrench my hand out of his grasp.

"Fine. Top of page forty-two. The Netherfield ball."

He arches a brow at me but doesn't comment as he flips to the right page.

Kyle glances back and forth between us, then bows his head and jumps off the edge of the stage, taking a seat in the first row.

He looks more disappointed than I thought he would.

I focus back on Beckett and begin. "I remember hearing you once say, Mr. Darcy, that you hardly ever forgave, that your resentment once created was unappeasable. You are very cautious, I suppose, as to its *being created*?"

Beckett stares at me, his gaze cold. "I am."

"And never allow yourself to be blinded by prejudice?" I ask, putting every ounce of anger and frustration and stress I've felt this morning into that single sentence.

"I hope not."

"It is particularly incumbent on those who never change their opinion, to be secure of judging properly at first."

He arches a brow, a small, pretentious smile twisting his lips. "May I ask to what these questions tend?"

I falter slightly under his gaze. "M-merely to the illustration of your character. I am trying to make it out."

"And what is your success?"

I'm not sure when it happens, but at some point, I stop trying to embarrass Beckett and really start listening to him. He's a natural—his expressions, his mannerisms, the way he places his inflections perfectly. It's subtle enough so as

not to be overdone, but not so subtle as to be unnoticeable.
He steps closer to me as my character tells him she's heard
so many different accounts of him, she can't make out who
the real Darcy is, and I'm so mesmerized by his stare that
I jumble all of my lines, even though they're right in front
of me, making it look like *I'm* the one who has no business
being on this stage, not him.

We say our last lines and, for a second, I'm so blown away,
I forget to breathe.

He smirks down at me like he knows just how good he
was, and that snaps me back to reality.

"Congratulations," I tell him. "You've got the part."

The entire room is silent. Only a single chair creaks.

Beckett blinks. "What?"

"You've got the part," I repeat. "You're our new Mr. Darcy."

"Ha. Yeah," he says, trying to hand me back the script. "I
don't think so."

"What's the matter?" I ask, forcing a firmness into my
voice I don't really feel. Beckett *has* to be Mr. Darcy. He was
the best one to audition by far. "Are you scared?"

"I'm busy."

"Oh yeah, you're real busy. Got another high school play
you need to go heckle?"

"And I'm not interested."

I arch a brow. "You seemed pretty interested when you
bounded up those steps like a Labrador."

"The only thing I was interested in was in proving you
wrong."

"Which you did," I tell him, "and now you're our new Mr.
Darcy. Congratulations."

"Would you stop saying that?"

"Saying what? That you're our new Mr. Darcy, or congratulations?"

"Both!"

His entire body is tense. Frustration pulses off him. Anyone in their right mind would be terrified of him in this moment, and yet I can't seem to stop.

"I would start memorizing your lines tonight if I were you. We only have three weeks until opening night."

"Not. Interested."

I gesture at the script he's holding between us like a shield. "I'm not taking that back. It's yours."

"It is not."

"Oh, and don't forget to give the costume department your measurements."

Beckett grits his teeth harder, sharpening the angles of his jaw so much, I'm pretty sure I could cut glass on them.

Mrs. Warren stands up. "Evelyn, dear, if the boy doesn't want to do it, then perhaps Kyle—"

"Don't worry, Mrs. Warren. I've got this," I tell her.

That chair in the audience squeaks again, and I realize it's Kyle, hunching forward in his seat. But before I can even begin to feel bad about unintentionally dismissing him, Beckett takes another step closer, so that the toes of our shoes are touching.

"Here's a little tip," he whispers, his voice rolling like thunder across my skin. "The quickest way to get me to *not* do something is to order me to do it."

"And here's a little tip from me," I say, not missing a beat. "If you didn't want to be cast in this play, you should've bombed your audition."

"I wasn't auditioning, I was—"

"And if you didn't want to audition," I continue, speaking over him, "you shouldn't have laughed at all of this in the first place. But you did laugh; and you did audition, and now you're in the play. Congratulations."

Becketts growls—*actually growls*—and heads down the stairs, slamming the script on the table in front of Mrs.

Warren. The collar of his coat sticks up around his ears as he grabs it from his seat and jams it on, stalking up the aisle and out the door.

No one says a word.

Aunt Bee clears her throat. "Well, I should get back to the store. People start talking if your lunch break takes longer than an hour." She stands and starts to follow Beckett, then turns back to me. "Do be sure to tell me if you need any more costumes or set pieces. I'm happy to see what I can find."

"I will, Aunt Bee. Thank you."

"And don't worry," she adds, a twinkle in her eye. "I'll make sure Beckett's costume fits him." And with that, she heads up the aisle and out the door.

And even though everyone else is staring at me like I've grown three additional heads, and Kyle is staring down at his shoes, looking like he's never been more disappointed in his life, it feels good to know that I have Aunt Bee in my corner.

Beckett Hawthorne is the best option we have. He *has* to play Darcy.

I won't have it any other way.

# 3

## Beckett

### ***

I slam open the school's lobby door, spilling out onto the snow-dusted courtyard. The cold air bites my knuckles. My nails cut crescents into my palms. My breathing is labored, my head is spinning, and my heart feels like it's going to beat out of my chest.

I push my hair out of my eyes. I need to get ahold of myself, to focus, to stop all of those old feelings from coming back, the ones that always show up whenever it feels like I'm being forced into a situation I can't control—ghosts of the past looming over me, laughing at me, pinning me down and choking the life out of me.

*Breathe*, the voice of my old violin teacher whispers in the back of my mind. *Focus. Ground yourself in where you are. Let go of everything else. Think only of the present moment.*

If I were in his study right now, holding my violin, he would tell me to feel the strings beneath my fingers, the grain of the bow in my hand. I haven't picked up my violin in years, but I lean into his methods anyway, measuring my breath, focusing on the crunch and grind of the snow beneath my feet.

The ghosts draw back, leaving only a vaguely unsettled feeling in their wake.

"Stupid," I mutter, brushing the fluffy powder off a courtyard bench and sitting down, my head in my hands.

I don't know what came over me back there. It's been so long since I laughed at anything that the sound escaping from my lips actually shocked me at first. I didn't even realize where it was coming from until Evelyn glared at me, but it was all so ridiculous—she had to see that, right? Ordering every boy in sight to audition for a role no one was interested in? And then, when they'd done their best to convince her that they had absolutely *no* business ever being on a stage in front of anyone, let alone *auditioning* to do so, it hadn't done a thing to discourage her.

Okay, so maybe it was a little cruel to laugh, especially the second time, but I wasn't laughing at her so much as at the situation—and at the fact that I've never met anyone so determined in my life.

I had no intention of auditioning. I even thought to myself, *No matter what she says, no matter what she does, when she flashes those sea-glass eyes at you, you are going to say no, you understand?* But then Kyle showed up, looking at her like a lost puppy, and something about imagining the two of them playing one of the most romantic couples in literary history set my teeth on edge. So, as I saw her lips forming the words, getting ready to say Kyle had the part, I jumped out of my seat and auditioned before I even knew what was happening.

I lay my head back against the bench, the snow seeping through the collar of my coat. "Idiot."

There's no way I'm going to be able to avoid Evelyn Waverley now. I wouldn't put it past her to hound me to play Darcy until the day I die.

The door *ka-thunks* behind me as Aunt Bee pushes it open.

"Don't say it," I tell her before she can open her mouth.

She shrugs. "Wasn't going to say anything. Ready to go?"

I push myself off the bench and head for her car. I try to hold onto the words Evelyn threw at me, the way she ordered me to play Darcy, echoing all the times in my life I haven't had a single say over what was happening to me, because holding onto the anger I felt in that moment seems better than the alternative—which is thinking about how, when Evelyn tilted her chin up at me, defying me, I'd had the sudden, overwhelming urge to run the pad of my thumb across her cheek—but the farther away we get from the school, the more the anger slips away, leaving a hollow ache in its place.

We make it halfway to the farmhouse before Aunt Bee says anything.

"You're going to do it, aren't you?" she asks.

I slide down in my seat, staring at the frozen fields outside my window. "Absolutely not."

"Hmm." She puts on her indicator and turns onto the interstate. "That's a shame."

I know she's waiting for me to ask why, but I don't to give her the satisfaction.

My cell rings.

Serena. My social worker.

"Hello?"

"Good afternoon, Mr. Hawthorne. How are you doing today?" she asks.

"Been better."

"Uh-oh. Sounds like someone woke up on the wrong side of the bed."

"Woke up fine," I tell her. "It's everything that's happened since that's the problem."

"Girl trouble?"

I turn my back on Aunt Bee. "In a sense."

"All right," she says, and I can picture her in her office, leaning back in her chair, her feet propped up on the edge of her desk. "What's the problem? Please tell me you didn't knock someone up."

I roll my eyes. "No."

"Give someone an STD?"

"No."

"*Get* an STD?"

"No!"

Aunt Bee glances at me.

"No," I say again, softer this time. "It's nothing like that."

"I can't help you if you don't help me, Mr. Hawthorne."

"Who said I need your help with this? All I need you to do is approve my community service hours and fill out whatever asinine paperwork the government uses to keep tabs on me until I turn eighteen. Which will happen in fifty-six days, by the way."

"Still planning on dropping out?"

"Yes," I reply. "Not that it's any of your business."

I don't know why I'm giving her such a hard time. I like Serena. She's one of the few people who's ever been kind to me, even if she's also re-homed me three different times over the last seven years. Logically, I know she was just doing her job to protect me, to find people to take me in while Mom worked on getting clean, but hearing her voice still makes me feel like I'm about to get the rug pulled out from under me, no matter how close I am to being done with it all.

"Everything you do from now until you turn eighteen is my business, Mr. Hawthorne, and as such, I'm going to do everything in my power to help you make the right decisions for your future. Now, setting that particular conversation aside for another time, tell me what has you so upset *today*."

Aunt Bee pulls into the gravel drive of the farmhouse.

"Some girl wants me to be in the school play," I murmur into the phone.

Serena pauses. "Did you audition?"

"Yes."

"And you were good?"

"I'm their only option."

"Yes, Serena," Aunt Bee says, leaning over the center console to speak into the receiver. "He was amazing. Like a young Marlon Brando."

I gesture at her to back off.

She huffs out a breath and flings her arms into the air, muttering, "Kids these days."

"It doesn't matter," I tell Serena. "I'm not doing it."

"Why?"

"Because it'll eat into my hours."

Another pause.

"What would you say," Serena replies slowly, "if I told you I think I can convince the judge to make it count? Would you do it then?"

"Not in a million years."

"I'm going to check anyway."

"I'd rather you didn't."

"Beckett."

She doesn't use my first name often. Unlike parents who use a child's full name when they've done something wrong or when they really need to pay attention, Serena only calls me Beckett if she believes something is in my best interest.

I lean back against the headrest and close my eyes. "Yeah?"

"You haven't been on a stage since the conservatory. I think it would be good for you. It might even help you pick up your violin again."

I hesitate. Then—my voice so soft, I'm not even sure if I'm saying it out loud or just thinking it—I ask, "What if I don't want to pick it up again?"

Serena exhales. "Just think about it. I'll let you know what the judge says."

She hangs up before I can argue.

I slide the phone back into my pocket.

"She's right, you know," Aunt Bee says.

"You are aware that eavesdropping is considered a *bad* thing, right?" I open my door and step out onto the drive.

"You should do the play," she calls after me. "It would be good for you."

I wave her away, closing the door. Her tires crunch snow-covered gravel as she kicks her car into reverse, heading back onto the interstate, shaking her head like she can't understand what's wrong with me.

The play—good for me? *Yeah, right.*

The only thing that's "good for me" is keeping a low profile and doing whatever I need to do to stay out of juvie.

Anything else has only ever gotten me into trouble.

### ✳✳✳

It's seven a.m. It's Monday. I'm groggy. And Evelyn Waverley is sitting at my kitchen table, looking way too alert for someone who's up before the sun. Her skin is dewy fresh, and her hair is curled this morning, half of it pulled back with a white ribbon that matches her fuzzy sweater. She looks like a cute, fluffy snowball. In contrast, I'm wearing my ratty old flannel pajama pants that are two inches too short on me and a T-shirt from a week-long, sixth-grade science camp my first foster family signed me up for.

"Good morning!" she practically shouts, the unadulterated joy in her voice giving me an instant headache.

I pause on the stairs, wincing. "Am I sleepwalking?"

"Nope!" Evelyn gestures to the white box sitting in the middle of the table. "I brought hot doughnuts. I wasn't sure what kind you liked, so I got one of each."

"Twenty-four in all," Uncle Bill says as he pulls a strawberry one out of the box. There's already a pile of chocolate crumbs on his plate and possibly the remains of a custard-filled one as well.

I absently run my hand through my hair, realizing too late that it's probably sticking up at weird angles now. I didn't sleep well—I haven't in years—and I know the circles under my eyes make me look like I spent the night at Fight Club instead of lying awake in bed. I don't have the energy for this, but I can't exactly turn around and go back up the stairs.

Can I?

Bill's staring at me like he'll cut me if I'm rude to this doughnut angel who has suddenly walked into our lives—so no, I definitely can't.

Pressing the palms of my hands into my eyes, I walk down the last few steps, taking the seat at the kitchen table across from Evelyn's.

"I also brought coffee," she says, revealing a second to-go cup next to hers.

She slides it to me, and before I can stop myself, the words "You *are* an angel" fall like flecks of gravel from my hoarse throat.

She looks down at the table, her cheeks turning pink.

I take a sip of the coffee. Usually I like my coffee black, but I don't hate the faint taste of peppermint in it. "Why are you here?"

"Well, that's a rude thing to ask someone who just brought you hot doughnuts," Uncle Bill mutters mid-chew.

I glare at him.

Evelyn sits up straighter. "I came to apologize."

"Well, that's a surprise."

"And to ask you to reconsider."

"Ah." I wrap my knuckles on the table. "There it is."

"You were right," she says, quickly. "I shouldn't have ordered you around. You just caught me on a bad day."

I make a *hmm* sound in the back of my throat, sounding just like Aunt Bee, albeit a grumpier version of her.

It must be genetic.

"But," she continues, "I don't think that's any reason to keep you from doing something you were clearly born to do."

"Oh yes, fulfilling my life-long dream of playing Mr. Darcy in a high school production of *Pride and Prejudice*. My parents will be so proud."

She rolls her eyes, and I can tell it's taking every ounce of control she has not to bite my head off. The knowledge that I can so easily get under her skin gives me more pleasure than it should.

"*No*," she says, stretching out the word. "What I *meant* was you were clearly born to perform. You came alive when you were on that stage. You must have felt it."

My fingers tingle as the memory of a glossy hardwood stage, recently polished, slams into my brain, and it's like I'm there, hot white lights beating down on me, a burst of applause rolling over me like a tidal wave. A feeling of rightness—of *purpose*—I haven't felt since...

I lean back in my chair. "I don't know what you mean."

I can feel Bill's eyes on me.

"Why don't you ask Kyle?" I lean forward, twisting my cup on the table. "He clearly wants to be the Darcy to your Elizabeth."

"What's that supposed mean?"

My lips twitch into a half smirk. "Nothing."

I don't know how she can be so in control of her sur-

roundings and yet so oblivious to the fact that Kyle Caldwell would give his right arm for a shot at her. He's not
the only one either. At least half the guys in school are in
love with her, but most of them are too intimidated to say
a single word to her, and the rest are too scared of what
Kyle will do to them if they try. But she has no clue. Maybe
that's why they all fall at her feet, because she doesn't even
realize what a catch she is.

Her eyes narrow. "If you *must* know—and it makes my
skin crawl to say this—Kyle doesn't hold a candle to you. I
offered him the role of understudy and a spot as an extra."
She leans forward, challenging me. "You are Darcy. Darcy
is you. Deal with it."

"Are you telling me," I say, slowly, "that I'm the carbon
copy of a man who is known for being an elitist, self-inter-
ested prick?"

"And one of the greatest romantic heroes ever written,"
she says, defending Darcy and unintentionally compliment-
ing me, making her eyes widen as she realizes it. "So." She
shifts uncomfortably in her seat. "Will you reconsider?"

I rap my knuckles on the table. "Don't think so, but thanks
for the grub." I reach for a cinnamon-apple doughnut with
cream cheese frosting. "See you at school?"

I expect her to look defeated, to finally give up, but
that's not Evelyn Waverley.

"Actually," she says, bright and cheery as ever, "I already
offered to drive you to school today."

I glance at Bill. "And you said...?"

"What? You think I don't have anything better to do
than drive you into town and back every morning?" He
grabs his plate, piling a plain, glazed doughnut on top of
his half-eaten strawberry one. "Now if you'll excuse me, I
believe *Match Game* is on."

I watch him grumble his way out of the kitchen, then

turn back to Evelyn. "I still have to get ready."

"I know."

"And finish eating breakfast."

"I know."

"And return the One Ring to Mordor."

"My, you do have a busy morning."

"Yes, and so, as you can see, it'd probably be best if I find my own way to school."

"That's all right. I'll just sit here and work on memorizing my lines while I wait." She pulls a copy of the script out of her bag. My gaze locks on the title (*A Pride and Prejudice Christmas*) and, for the first time, I notice the words *by Evelyn Waverley* written underneath. She leans back in her chair and doesn't look at me as she adds, "Tell Samwise I said hello."

I set the doughnut back down, no longer hungry. Now I get why she's so obsessed with this thing. She wrote it— an *entire* play. I can't even find time to write a six-hundred-word essay on *Beowulf,* and yet here she is adapting a nineteenth-century novel for the stage while being senior class president, participating in three different clubs, volunteering in every charity known to man, and—I don't know—probably saving lost puppies from city dumpsters in her spare time.

*Evelyn Waverley,* I think as I stare at her, my gaze traveling over the leg she's propped up on the edge of her chair to the little furrow in her brow that she gets every time she's concentrating on something. *No wonder half the school's in love with you.*

"You're not going to bother me about the play the whole way to school, are you?" I ask, shoving that particularly unwelcome thought aside.

"I wouldn't dream of it," she replies, not looking up from her script.

I don't believe her for a second.

I sigh and dust the crumbs off my hands. "Fine. I'll be back in twenty."

"Are we really so close to Mordor that you can get there and back in twenty minutes?"

"You're not funny," I tell her as I head back up the stairs.

"Keep an eye out for Gollum," she calls back. "Don't let him steal the precious."

I shake my head but a smile cuts into my cheeks, and I'm thankful my back is to her so she can't see it.

After taming my hair, I throw on a pair of jeans and an old blue hoodie that's seen better days, my gaze catching on the black case gathering dust in the closet. Something tugs at the pit of my stomach, and I suddenly hate the play—and Evelyn Waverley—even more, for making me wish for things I've long since buried.

Uncle Bill is lying back in his recliner when I return, watching the Game Show Network, and Evelyn is still sitting at the kitchen table, her eyes closed as she softly murmurs lines under her breath. She's so focused on what she's doing, she doesn't even hear me walk up to her.

I tap her on the shoulder.

She nearly jumps out of her seat.

"Ready?" I ask, in an even fouler mood than before.

She frowns at my tone. "You sure you don't want another doughnut first? We have time."

"It feels like a bribe and therefore unsafe."

"How suspicious you are."

"And yet how correct."

She stands and waves at Bill. "Thanks for having me, Mr. Campbell."

"Not a problem," he replies. "You just bring some more of those delicious doughnuts again, you hear?"

"There won't be any more doughnuts," I call back to him

while keeping my eyes pointedly on her, "because Evelyn is
a very busy girl who doesn't have time to pick us up breakfast every morning—"

"You've got it, Mr. Campbell," she yells to him over my
shoulder before turning on her heel and heading for the
mudroom.

I grit my teeth as I follow her out of the kitchen and
through the front door. It snowed again last night, another
two inches, and the patch of powder covering the front
yard and gravel drive is painted amber gold in the glow of
the porch lights.

Evelyn's white boots—whose shallow treads appear to
be more fashionable than functional—slip on the top step.
There's a sharp intake of breath as she pitches forward. I
wrap my hand around her arm and pull her back against
me. Her spine slams into my chest, forcing out an *"Oof"*.
The apricots-and-honey scent of her shampoo makes my
head spin. As does the way her body, just for a moment,
melts into mine.

She looks back at me, breathless. "Thanks."

I clear my throat. "Don't mention it."

I hold on to her elbow, helping her down the steps, and
there's an ache in my chest I can't explain when she reaches
the bottom and I let her go. And that messes with my head
too—the fact that I can go from being completely pissed at
her, to wanting to run my fingers through her hair.

*What the hell is wrong with me?*

An old-school Volkswagen bug sits in our driveway, looking clean and polished, with just a small crust of salt on the
bumper from the interstate.

"Whoa." I stop. "Is this your car?"

She nods. "I fixed it up with my grandpa a few summers
ago. He bought it cheap at a used-car lot. It needed a lot
of work but helping him find the right parts taught me so

much about cars. We even replaced the seats and repainted the exterior. Someone in the seventies painted it burnt orange with a brown leather interior." She shudders. "It still gives me nightmares."

I laugh as I run my fingers along the gleaming silver trim. The white leather seats match the steering wheel, and the silver accents on the dashboard are just as polished as the exterior trim.

"It's beautiful," I whisper.

I've always admired cars. Probably because during the rare months Mom had a working car, ours was always some rusted-out beater one pothole away from crumbling into a pile of dust. I didn't even realize cars like this existed until my second foster family took me to a car show. Their dad was really into Firebirds, but I preferred the older models: rounded, bulbous trucks from the fifties that looked like they belonged in a Norman Rockwell painting; the 1930s Oldsmobiles the Prohibition gangsters drove around in; and a 1922 Rolls-Royce Silver Ghost, painted yellow for the original *Great Gatsby* movie.

I walked around those cars and decided that one day, I would own something that beautiful. Own it outright, paid in full, so no one could ever take it away.

Evelyn doesn't say anything as I walk around her car now, taking in every curve. The sky is lightening on the horizon behind her, pitch black to dark sapphire, and suddenly I'm not looking at the car at all. I'm looking at her—at the way the porch light cups the side of her face, liquid-gold against ivory skin, as she stares at her car, lost in memories that make her lips pull into the most radiant smile I've ever seen.

She looks up. If she's surprised to see me staring at her, or if she realizes the effect she's having on me, she doesn't show it.

"Ready?" she asks.

I nod.

I open the passenger side door, tapping the snow from my boots before sliding in, but it turns out I didn't need to. White plastic weather mats cover the floor, which seems like such an Evelyn Waverley thing to do that it makes me laugh. I'm also not surprised to find that her car is immaculately clean. Not even a receipt in the center console from her bakery run this morning, even though the air still smells of fried dough and melted sugar.

Evelyn throws her pink backpack into the backseat, another thing about her that feels too cheery this early in the morning. I hesitate to do the same. My backpack, which I've had since middle school and is now more duct tape and coffee stains than fabric, suddenly seems filthy by comparison.

Uncle Bill offered to buy me a new one, but I told him no, my tone colder than I meant for it to be. I just hate feeling like I'm indebted to anyone, which I have been my whole life. The only reason I'm alive is because of people like Serena, Uncle Bill and Aunt Bee, and even my foster families. They've done enough for me as it is—I don't need to add anything else to their plates. But now, a part of me wishes I had taken him up on it.

Luckily, a stronger part of me recognizes this is for the best. I need to remember that Evelyn and I come from two completely different worlds, ones that should never orbit each other for fear that I might tarnish the brilliance of her planet with the darkness of my own.

I place my backpack between my feet, melted snow bleeding from my boots into the blue fabric peeking around the duct-taped corners.

Evelyn has the decency to wait until she pulls out of the driveway and onto the interstate before mentioning the play again, a whole ninety seconds longer than I expected her to.

"So," she begins, flicking on her indicator and turning toward town, "what exactly do you have against the play?"

"I don't have anything against it."

"Okay, let me rephrase. What do you have against being *in* the play?"

"I told you. I'm just not interested."

"What can I do to *make* you interested?"

My eyes slide to her lips before I can stop myself. I force them back on the road, hoping she didn't notice. "Nothing."

"Come on," she says. "There has to be something. Now I know you love coffee—"

"Me? Hate the stuff. Never drink it."

"You called me an angel when I gave it to you."

"I was sleepwalking. I didn't know what I was saying."

"Mm-hmm." She makes another turn, this one onto Cherry Street, heading toward the town square. "What if I bring you coffee every morning? Would you be in the play then?"

"Not a chance."

"Coffee and...bagels?"

I shake my head.

"Cookies?"

"No."

"Cake? Pie? A breakfast sandwich?"

"No, no, and no."

"You're saying you don't like any of those things?"

"I'm saying I don't like any of those things enough to get me up on a stage ever again."

She pauses. "Again?"

*Crap.* I didn't mean to say that part.

"Just forget it," I tell her.

"But—"

"Even if I wanted to, I don't have the time, so just drop it, okay?"

She lets out a long, slow breath through her teeth, thinking.

"I'd love to drop it," she says finally, "but I can't. I spent all summer writing this script. I can't give it up now just because one of our leads broke his leg doing something stupid."

"The video?"

She nods.

*Don't ask*, I think. *Don't give her any reason to believe you're interested in a single aspect of this play.*

But the question shoots out of my mouth before I can stop it.

"Why *did* you write the script? Is that what you want to do with your life? Write plays?"

She looks at me, probably surprised I'm actually holding a conversation with her. It's not my norm, and I'm already kicking myself for asking.

"I, uh, well." She takes a deep breath. "I want to get into an Ivy League, like my mom and my aunt, but I need something to make my application stand out. I thought being able to say that I wrote, starred in, and co-directed a play based on a British classic might do the trick. Plus, I love Jane Austen. Have you read any of her books?"

"I'm more of a Jack Kerouac fan myself."

Evelyn snorts. "Figures."

"What's that supposed to mean?"

"Fits your vibe, is all." She stares hard at the road. "Seriously though. What can I do to change your mind?"

I'm about to tell her, "Nothing," but my phone buzzes, stopping me. A text from Serena.

*Judge okayed the play. It'll count toward your community service hours. Have fun!* ☺

I lean my head back against the seat and groan. "What the hell is wrong with the women in my life?"

Evelyn blinks. "I don't even know how to respond to that."

"Hold on. Just...let me think."

I hadn't planned on ever doing anything on a stage ever again, but the Christmas-tree lot is only open until five on the weekdays and from ten to four on Saturdays, so between school and homework, it can be hard to rack up the hours I need as quickly as I would like.

"How often do you rehearse?" I ask.

"Three hours a day, every day after school, and from eight to noon on Saturdays."

I do a quick mental calculation. By the time I get home from school, I only get an hour of worktime at the lot before it closes, which means I'll get ten more a week rehearsing instead. I'll also get two extra hours on Saturdays if I go to rehearsal at eight and then work at the lot from noon to four. Which means by opening night, I'll have sixty-one hours completed of the eighty-two I have left, plus however many hours I'll rack up by actually performing in the play that weekend. If I only worked at the lot in the same amount of time, I'd get thirty-three.

I can't believe what I'm about to do.

I close my eyes tight and, like ripping off a Band-Aid, say, "Fine. I'll be in the play."

Evelyn spins her head toward me so fast, I'm surprised she doesn't get whiplash. "What?"

"I said I'll do it. I'll be your Mr. Darcy."

# 4

## Evelyn

### ✳✳✳

I sla and Savannah both thought I was crazy when I told them over FaceTime that I was going to get Beckett to play Mr. Darcy or die trying.

"We're still talking about Beckett Hawthorne, right?" Isla had asked. It was Saturday night, several frustrating hours after Beckett's audition and subsequent refusal to play Darcy, and Isla's coppery red hair was up in an impressive topknot, curly tendrils framing her face and brushing the white Peter Pan collar of the dress she always wore when working. A wedding reception was in full swing behind her, with multicolored lights sweeping the room and a DJ pumping a dizzying mixture of mid-2000s pop and punk rock in the background. Her mom, Lorna Riddle, owns the fastest-growing wedding planning business on the entire East Coast, along with the bridal boutique in the old firehouse. Every Saturday is completely booked for Isla from now into eternity if she decides to go full-time at her mom's office right out of high school, and considering she loves everything to do with weddings and romance and fairy-tale endings, I don't see any reason why she wouldn't. "Our school didn't get some new Beckett I'm not aware of?"

"The same one," I replied.

"So, let me get this straight," Savannah said, flipping the page on her physics textbook and jotting something down. "Dude laughs at your passion, and you offer him the lead role?"

She was spread out on her bed with homework, college applications, and who knew what else surrounding her. Her laptop faced the wall behind her bed, so I could see the posters of her favorite bands she had meticulously lined up to look like expensive wallpaper. This was also a typical Saturday night for Savannah—her mom had her when she was sixteen, and Savannah, diagnosed with dyslexia at age seven, is determined to prove every statistic wrong, get into a good school, and do something amazing with her life. Explore undiscovered ruins in the Amazon rainforest. Scale Mount Kilimanjaro. Decipher ancient languages and learn the secrets of the universe, and then write endless books about her travels, discoveries, and just how generally amazing her life is. Isla and I both know she's going to do it. She's the type of person who will do whatever someone tells her she *can't* do.

For my part, I had already finished my homework Tuesday night, before Thanksgiving break even started, so I was obsessively reorganizing my closet to keep myself from marching over to Beckett Hawthorne's house and camping out in his front yard until he agreed to play Darcy.

"I know it's ridiculous," I told them as I rearranged my spring Keds by color instead of most-to-least used, making a pastel rainbow on the second row of my shoe rack. "I mean, I must be completely out of my mind, but he really is that good. I can't imagine anyone else playing him."

And then Isla got that familiar goofy smile on her face and that "true love" twinkle in her eye. "You know—"

"Don't say it."

"It *is* kind of romantic."

Savannah shook her head and muttered something under her breath, her pencil flying over a calculation in her notebook. If Isla is fairy-tale romances and Happily Ever Afters, Savannah is cold, hard statistics and sensible practicality. Savannah swears it has nothing to do with the supposed curse that has kept the women in her family from finding true love for generations (superstitious nonsense in her opinion), and everything to do with not letting an immature boy keep her from achieving her dreams, but Isla and I suspect the real reason is that she's seen her mom's heart shatter one too many times and doesn't ever want to go through the same, seemingly unbearable pain.

I usually fall somewhere in the middle of the two, often playing referee in the Benefits of True Love vs. Single Womanhood Debate, but this time, I was squarely on Savannah's side.

"It's not like that," I told Isla through gritted teeth.

"But an audition is the perfect 'meet cute'!" Isla replied.

"Trust me, nothing was cute about that 'meet'. I would've scratched his eyes out when he looked at me with that dumb, smug smile if they hadn't been so perfectly Darcy-ish. It still pisses me off that he *knows* how good he was."

"Also very Darcy-ish," Savannah mumbled, flipping back a page. Neither Vanna nor Isla has read *P&P*, but I've made them both watch every movie adaptation more times than I can count.

"Exactly," I said.

Isla chewed on her bottom lip. "But you have to admit—"

"I DON'T HAVE TO ADMIT ANYTHING," I yelled, accidentally flinging a sandal across the room.

I spent my entire Sunday devising my battle plan, then set an extra-early 5:00 a.m. alarm this morning so I could get to Beckett's house with hot-from-the-oven dough- nuts—something I thought I was going to have to do every day this week to make him crack, which is why I narrow my eyes at him now as the light ahead of me turns red and I press on the brake.

This must be a trick.

"Why?" I ask.

"None of your business."

*Stop, Evelyn. You got what you wanted. Leave it alone.*

Except I can't leave it alone. There's more to his story—I have to know what it is.

The light turns green. The high school is two blocks ahead of us. We enter the line waiting to turn into the parking lot.

"You know what?" I say. "I've changed my mind. I'd rather have Kyle do it."

"Suit yourself."

I blow out a breath. "Okay, that was a lie. I just wanted to see if you were more interested than you were letting on."

He sits up and locks eyes with me, his hair slashing across his temples. "Look, I'm not some puzzle you need to solve, and I'm definitely not some project you need to take on. I don't need to be in your play—I don't even want to *be* in your play—but I'll do it just to get you to stop talking about it. Got it?"

"Got it," I repeat. The car ahead of me moves forward a couple inches, and I ease up on the brake. "But just to be clear, I *will* be talking to you about the play for the next three weeks. That's kind of my job. Co-director and all."

"Yeah, but at least I know you won't show up at my house with doughnuts at seven o'clock every morning."

"No promises."

He mutters something under his breath.

I chew on my bottom lip, a nervous habit. "Do you think you'll be able to memorize all of your lines in three weeks?"

"Don't worry about it."

*Shut up, Evelyn. Shut up, shut up, shut—*

"Because Greg was three weeks into rehearsals and he *still* didn't have them memorized, even though Darcy has half the number of lines that Elizabeth does—"

"I said don't worry about it."

"Fine."

"Splendid."

I turn into the parking lot, grabbing a spot by the auditorium.

"Rehearsal is at three o'clock," I tell him as his fingers curl around the door handle. "Don't be late."

"Wouldn't dream of it," he murmurs back in a way that sounds like he very much *will* dream of it and that I shouldn't hold my breath expecting him to be on time for a single rehearsal.

I watch him stalk into the school ahead of me, wisps of cottony snow drifting down around him. He keeps his head down and his hands in his pockets, putting off serious "Don't talk to me" vibes, and even though I hate the fact that our play is now relying on Beckett Hawthorne of all people, I have to admit that as far as personality and temperament go, we couldn't have picked a better Darcy.

✳✳✳

I stand in the middle of the auditorium, breathing in the sights and sounds of chaos and commotion swirling around me as our cast huddles together, some sharing after-school snacks from the vending machine as they go over lines, others working on set design, painting a starry back-drop for the ballroom scenes, or practicing box steps for the authentic Regency dances Sarah has been researching for weeks. Jeremy needs notes on lighting for the third act, and Mrs. Warren is asking me whether we should streamline the second act by combining a few scenes, and I have never felt more in my element.

People make fun of me for it, but I love being in the mid-dle of a bustling puzzle with moving pieces for me to solve. I love feeling productive. Love seeing the cause-and-effect results that come from my direction. Love motivating people to pull off something bigger together than they could have ever done by themselves. Love seeing a project through from beginning to end and then immediately looking for the next thing I can sink my teeth into.

And no matter how many people tell me I'm too passion-ate or too driven or too pushy (which, let's be honest, is just a sexist way of saying *persistent*), I have to believe that when a person finds that thing that makes them feel completely alive, they have to hold onto it and not let anyone tell them it's "too" anything. Which is why I cram my schedule to the breaking point. I *live* for keeping all my plates spinning in the air, never letting a single one drop.

I answer Mrs. Warren's and Jeremy's questions; consult Graham and Piper about the staging for the opening scene; check in with our costume department about a dress that needs to be altered for Jen, while Patrick, my stage manag-er, brings a paper for me to sign, accepting delivery of the two fake snow machines that are going to be placed on the catwalk over the stage; and then I head back into the main auditorium, clapping my hands to get everyone's attention.

"Listen up."

Conversations peter out as everyone turns toward me. My gaze catches on Kyle, who stopped by my locker before first period to ask if Beckett had decided to take the role.

"He did," I informed him. "This morning."

Kyle's entire face fell. "Oh."

"I'm sorry," I said quickly, surprised for the second time at his genuine disappointment. Who knew Kyle Caldwell was so into theater?

"It's okay," he replied. "I'm just excited to be in it, even if I am only the understudy."

I exhaled. "Yeah, well, you better start working on practicing those lines. I'm not holding my breath that Beckett Hawthorne will actually show up for any of the rehearsals, let alone opening night. He doesn't exactly strike me as reliable."

"Is that important to you? Being reliable?" he asked.

"In a play where everyone is counting on you? Yeah. It's important."

"I meant, uh, *personally*. You know, like...in a boyfriend?"

My brow furrowed. Kyle had been acting so weird lately, but it felt kind of rude to ask him if he'd taken one too many hits to the head this season. "Um, yeah. It is."

He stood up straighter. "I'm reliable."

I closed my locker. "Just another reason why all of Christmas High loves you."

He cleared his throat. "Not all."

"They're building a shrine to you in the courtyard for taking the team to State two years in a row," I teased. "You didn't notice?"

He laughed, but it sounded kind of strangled. "It's just that...well, there's this one girl in particular who—"

The bell rang.

"Crap, I'm going to be late to Pre-Calc." I lunged forward, glancing over my shoulder at him as I headed for the stairs. "See you at rehearsal?"

He nodded. "Wouldn't miss it."

Now, he's sitting forward with his elbows on his knees

and his hands clasped in front of him, hanging on my every word, unlike Beckett, who has his English textbook open to *Beowulf* and is scribbling furiously in his notebook.

I clear my throat. Loudly.

Beckett glances up, unimpressed.

I cock my head at him. "We're going to be rehearsing the breakfast-parlor scene at Netherfield, when Mrs. Bennet comes to check on Jane. So I need *Darcy*,"—I say his name extra pointedly—"Mr. and Miss Bingley, Mrs. Bennet, Lydia, and Kitty on stage, please."

Everyone bounds up the stairs to join me.

Everyone but Beckett.

He gets up from his seat slowly, like he's not entirely sure what he's gotten himself into. He's wearing a tattered blue hoodie that's tight across his chest and sags a little around his tapered waist, and I try not to notice the way the fabric hugs his biceps, or the way it pulls taut across his shoulders. The hoodie looks like something from a past life, something that used to fit him but doesn't anymore, and I wonder why he hasn't replaced it. Aunt Bee mentioned he's been working at the farm, so he must have the money for a new one, unless he's saving it for something else?

There's a question in Beckett's eyes as he moves toward me, and I realize I've been staring at him without meaning to.

I look away. "Let's start from the top, with Mrs. Bennet's line."

I feel Beckett watching me as our Mrs. Bennet begins, saying that her daughter Jane is too ill to be moved from the Bingleys' home at Netherfield, which is really a ploy to get her daughter to spend more time with the very rich—and very available—Mr. Bingley. I stare hard at my script as if I don't have every line memorized.

Finally, Beckett looks down at his script, and I can breathe again.

When it's Beckett's turn to speak, he stumbles a little over the first line and says it much too softly. If he were anyone else, I'd remind him to project, but considering Beckett is the best Darcy we have and he already looks spooked, I decide to leave it for now and bring it up later, when everyone's packing up to leave and not paying any attention to us.

He clears his throat and delivers his second line a little stronger than the first: "In a country neighborhood you move in a very confined and unvarying society."

"But people themselves alter so much," I reply, "that there is something new to be observed in them forever."

Beckett meets my gaze, and, not for the first time, my breath catches at the way he looks at me, like he sees something other people don't.

I really wish he would stop doing that.

"I cannot see that London has any great advantage over the country, for my part," our Mrs. Bennet says pompously, just as she should, and I'm not sure how or when it happens but Beckett eases into the scene. His body relaxes, and he begins having genuine reactions to Mrs. Bennet—small reactions, almost imperceptible, which are perfect for Darcy, who is the epitome of tightly controlled emotions—and for the first time since Greg Bailey fell down those stairs and broke his leg in three places, I feel like we might actually have a chance at pulling this thing off.

# 5

## Beckett

***

*E*veryone's laughing and joking about the play, groaning about all of the homework waiting for them when they get home, or discussing strategies for some video game they're going to meet up on later as they grab their things and shuffle in groups out of the auditorium. Meanwhile I'm stuffing my script into my backpack and frowning at the corner of paper that peeks out of a hole in the bottom no matter how many times I take it out and jam it back in. I make a mental note to duct-tape the entire thing before it disintegrates on me.

Evelyn's sitting in the second row, just across the aisle from me, using a green pen to mark something in her script, while two more pens—red and blue—wait to be used in her other hand, and a purple one rests behind her ear. The sleeves of her sweater are pushed up to her elbows, revealing a dusting of freckles on her arms. Her rings—one on her left ring finger and two thin circlets on her right thumb—glint in the antique lighting as she works, and suddenly I feel like I'm seeing a glimpse of Future Evelyn, the one writing important legal briefs in an upscale law office or going over accounts for a world-changing organization.

No one can look at Evelyn Waverley and not see a girl bursting to set the world on fire.

I wonder what it would be like to see inside her brain, to observe all the connections she's making, the ideas spilling out onto the page. Her pen, her thoughts, her words move quickly, like she's trying not to lose track of them all, but there's nothing frenetic about it. It's controlled. Intentional. Magnetic. In fact, the only time I've ever seen Evelyn Waverley flustered was the other day, when she needed to find a new Darcy. Other people who don't look at her too closely might think she's flustered all the time, simply because chaos seems to swirl around her, but I've watched her enough to know she doesn't get bowled over by the maelstrom. It doesn't pull her down like an undertow—it circles her like planets orbiting the sun. And just like the sun, she keeps everything spinning in alignment, her very nature a gravitational pull that keeps every part moving exactly as it should.

It's mesmerizing to watch, and I've had to remind myself several times to stop staring at her so much, but for someone who's never had a single ounce of control in his life, I can't help wondering what it must be like to be her—or, better yet, to be pulled into her gravitational sphere. Set in alignment. Taken care of. No more getting jerked around from foster family to foster family or from a strung-out mom in Texas to an aunt and uncle I barely knew, who'd taken me in out of—what? A sense of charity? Familial obligation? Just because they're good people and it was the right thing to do?

I have no doubt that if Evelyn Waverly could take over my life for even just one day, she'd find some way to sort it all out, and that in and of itself makes me feel like a moth being pulled toward her flame, even though I am as flimsy and inconsequential as paper and it's only a matter of time before I catch fire and burn.

One by one, everyone leaves, until it's just the two of us.

*Stop staring.*

I look away. At the floor, the chairs, the ceiling.

*Why am I not leaving?*

I clear my throat without meaning to.

She turns her head to look at me, her eyes wide. "Did everyone leave already?"

I nod.

She leans back in her chair. "I didn't even notice."

I tell myself to leave, but I take the seat in front of her instead, resting my arm on the chairback. "Anything I can help with?"

She angles her body toward me. "Why?"

"Because, believe it or not, I am, at times, a fairly helpful fellow."

She snorts. "I'll believe it when I see it."

"I'm doing the play, aren't I?"

"After much cajoling by yours truly." She crosses a line out of her script with red ink.

"And doughnuts. Don't forget about the doughnuts."

She switches back to the green pen. "You said you didn't like doughnuts."

"I never said I didn't like doughnuts. I just said they weren't enticing enough to tempt me."

She shakes her head, amazed. "You really are the perfect Darcy."

"Considering your character refers to him as being 'haughty, reserved, fastidious' and 'continually giving offense', I'm not sure that's a compliment."

"Trust me, it is. Darcy is one of the most romantic heroes ever written. There are a lot worse people you could be compared to."

I blink, not sure how to take the fact that this is the second time she's said this to me today.

She blushes and taps her pen against her script, leaving little emerald dots along the edge. "I should get back to this."

"Seriously, I'd like to help. If I can."

She stares at me like she's trying to figure me out, and I would love to know what she sees when she looks at me. If she can sort me out just as clearly and concisely as she does everything else.

"The pacing's a bit slow in the second act," she finally tells me, "and there are currently seven scenes that need completely different set designs, but we only have enough money left in our budget for three. So I'm trying to figure out how to combine them."

I place my backpack on the floor and shrug out of my coat, twisting around to face her more fully. "All right, let's see what you've got so far."

Her brow furrows. "You really want to help?"

I nod. "I haven't finished reading the book yet, so I'm not as well versed as you are in what should happen, but I'm a great sounding board if you need one."

The room is so quiet, there is nothing in the space between my offer and her answer but the hum of the heating vents and the soft catch of her breath.

"You're reading the book?" she asks.

"Was I not supposed to?"

The fact that I'm teasing her registers in my brain in a distant sort of way. It's been so long since I've teased anyone, since I've felt the joy and ease to do so, that the act feels foreign even as the words drip like honey from my tongue.

"Are you liking it?"

"Yes," I say, softly. "Very much."

I watch her throat work as she swallows, my eyes tracing her ivory skin and the sharp line of her clavicle disappearing into her puffy white sweater.

"Um, yeah," she says, leaning forward so that our brows are only a few inches apart as we stare down at the marked-up script. "I'd love a sounding board right about now."

"At your service."

She smiles. Quick, then gone. But I noticed.

And I don't know why, but I want to make her do it again.

\* \* \*

# 6
## Evelyn

\*\*\*

*B*eckett smells like the Christmas tree farm. Pine needles and snow-dampened bark and cold winter air. His hair is falling into his eyes again, and he pushes it back with a hand that looks long enough to palm a basketball, all sharp bones and taut veins. He has the kind of hands an artist could spend their entire life drawing and never grow tired of.

I almost ask him about the calluses on his fingertips, but before I can open my mouth, he asks, "What's up with the different pens?" gesturing to my script.

"It's my system," I tell him, clearing my throat. "Green for set design; red for characterization; blue for staging; purple for miscellaneous."

He smiles.

"What?"

"Nothing. I've just never met anyone so organized in my life. It's cute."

My eyes widen.

He looks away.

"So," he says, his voice softer. "What scenes are you trying to combine?"

"That's a good question." I alternate between the blue, red, and green pens as I dissect each scene in the second act, explaining which ones I think we can cut down and combine with others.

"I don't know that the walking scenes at Pemberley are crucial," I say, "but we definitely need Elizabeth touring Pemberley, and maybe we can find some way to show Elizabeth and Darcy spending time in the house instead of on the grounds? Although that'll be hard to figure out because showing her aunt and uncle the grounds is the whole reason Darcy spends that much time with Elizabeth in the first place..."

Beckett listens attentively, letting me talk in circles. Everyone I know gets annoyed with me in two seconds flat when I do this, but it's literally the only way my brain can untangle a problem and put the pieces back together in the right order, and Beckett doesn't seem to mind. He asks questions here and there, helping me focus the overall picture into the most crucial scenes. Soon there are flow charts and pro/con lists and whole chunks of dialogue crossed out or condensed so that only the most necessary information remains. At one point, Beckett vaults over the back of his chair to grab the seat next to mine, our arms resting against each other as he helps me reconstruct the scene where Elizabeth learns that Darcy is the one who saved her family from scandal (after her sister Lydia ran off, *unmarried*, with Wickham). He doesn't seem to think anything of it, as if our skin touching from wrist to elbow is the most natural thing in the world, while I am so hyperaware of his arm against mine that my brain gets muddled and I can't think of anything else until I purposely pull it away.

I'm sure Isla would have something to say about that. Savannah too, although she would go on about teenage hormones and chemical proximity, while Isla would wax poetic about true love and soul mates and fairy-tale endings.

I think my brain just doesn't know how to handle being so close to someone I've decided to hate. It also doesn't know what to do with the fact that Beckett is actually helping. Scenes are coming together. The pace is flowing. And I have Beckett Hawthorne—of all people—to thank.

An hour later, my stomach is growling, and my fingers are cramping, but I'm grinning from ear to ear. "I can't believe it." I close the script and take a deep breath, feeling a thousand pounds lighter. "We actually managed to combine everything in a way that makes sense."

"What do you mean, 'we'?" he asks. "I was just here for moral support. That was all you."

My cheeks warm as I put the caps back on the pens, stuffing them into my backpack along with my script.

"Forgot one," he says, reaching up and slowly—*gently*—pulling the purple pen out from behind my ear.

I reach for the pen, my fingertips brushing his. "Thanks."

He gives me that half smirk again, the one that instantly brings to mind Hollywood bad boys and rock 'n' roll legends. "No problem."

My stomach growls again.

"Hungry?"

Heat encircles my cheeks. Seriously, how many times am I going to blush around him? "Starving."

"Me too."

Don't ask. He's the *last* person you want to grab food with.

Except, this past hour was...nice. Not like anything I've ever experienced with Beckett before. And I'd be lying if I said I wasn't curious about him. Which must be why the words "You wouldn't want to grab some food with me, would you?" tumble out of my mouth, even as my brain is shouting: *WHAT ARE YOU DOING? HE'S THE ENEMY.*

"Uh, yeah," he says, blinking. "Sure."

And that is how Beckett Hawthorne ends up back in the passenger seat of my car, streetlights flashing over him as we drive through the center of town. I try not to notice every breath, every shift of his long legs as he moves and stretches and pushes the seat back to give himself more room, but it's impossible. He takes up more space than just the seat he occupies, like every single thing in this car has been made smaller in response to the largeness of him, and a question echoes in the back of my mind:

When did Beckett Hawthorne become so hard to ignore?

# 7

## Beckett

### ***

*E*velyn takes me to Nora's, an old-fashioned ice cream parlor on Main Street squashed between a small accounting firm and what looks like a wedding planner's office, which sits adjacent to a wedding dress shop in an old firehouse. The sign hanging over the door reads, *Wedding Starting to Feel Like a Riddle? We'll Solve It for You!*

Evelyn notices me staring at it as we walk by.

"My best friend's mom owns that business and the bridal boutique next door," she says. "It's getting really popular. They're even being featured in *Southern Fried Weddings* this month."

I have no idea what *Southern Fried Weddings* is, but it sounds like a big deal, so I nod and say, "Cool."

Icicles dangle from every store awning, reflecting the white Christmas lights that swirl up the old-fashioned lampposts lining the street, while circles of gold-dappled light puddle and pool atop snowy crevices and ice lying in sheets on the road where the salt didn't reach.

"She's really talented," Evelyn says.

"The mom?"

"No," she replies. "I mean yes, but no, I meant my friend. Isla Riddle? She's a year younger than us, so you may not know her." Her toe kicks an oversized salt cube that goes tumbling down the sidewalk. "She's a total romance junkie, and she thinks every meet cute should end in a happily ever after."

"I'm sorry—'meet cute'?"

Evelyn smiles, embarrassed. "It's when a couple meets in a really cute way. Like when two people aren't looking where they're going, so they bump into each other and papers go flying, and their hands touch while gathering everything up and they suddenly realize they're soul mates?"

"Seems like something that would lead to a higher incidence of ER visits instead of a happily ever after."

She laughs, but her face is screwed up in that way it gets when she's thinking really hard about something. "Yeah, I guess so. Or maybe I'm just not explaining it right. There's also the elevator meet cute, the sharing-the-same-cab meet cute, or, Isla's personal favorite, the dog park meet cute—" She cuts herself off. "Sorry. I'm babbling."

I stare at her, mystified. I've never seen her this nervous. Am *I* making her this nervous?

"So." I clear my throat. "Does your friend believe happily-ever-afters are only reserved for those couples who 'meet cute', or can people meet in an average way and still have a fairy-tale ending?"

"Jury's still out on that, I'm afraid. My other friend, Savannah, is the total opposite. She thinks romance is just a bunch of hormones and chemicals firing off in someone's brain and that it doesn't really mean anything."

"What do you think?" For some reason I can't explain, the answer matters to me, although I'm not sure what it is I want her to say.

She looks down at the ground. "I know my parents are in love. They met their first day in college. Their dorms were across from each other. Kind of cute, I guess, but nothing epic. They fight sometimes, but they also still cuddle on the couch every night after dinner, so I think that's become my definition of happily ever after. Not finding this imaginary romance where you never fight and things are always perfect but finding someone you never want to be too far away from. Someone you want to cuddle with every night, even twenty years in."

I nod. "Sounds like a good definition to me."

Our breath fans out in front of us as we climb the three steps up to the parlor's door, painted turquoise with the address written in calligraphy across the middle and a silver wreath hanging above it. White Christmas lights frame the bay window overlooking the street and the snow-covered square beyond.

It's blessedly warm inside. We stomp our boots on the weather mats in front of the door so as not to track snow and salt across the black-and-white checkered floor. A short hallway opens up into a larger room with antique café tables and chairs and servers standing behind an ice cream bar, wearing white aprons and those old-fashioned paper hats. There are cakes, cookies, and pastries in the display case alongside tubs of mint chocolate chip, Neapolitan, Rocky Road, and every other ice cream flavor imaginable. Evelyn moves toward the bar as a little boy toddles past me, carrying a candy cane in both hands. His older brother follows him, making sure he doesn't fall. The boy takes a sudden turn, and his brother swoops his arms around him, pulling him back a tenth of a second before he cracks his head on a table corner.

The little boy laughs and stares up at his brother like

he did it on purpose, just so he could fall into something safe, and my heart squeezes painfully at the knowledge that no matter where that little boy goes—no matter what he does—someone cares what happens to him.

"Beckett?"

I glance at Evelyn. "Yeah?"

"It's your turn to order."

"Um—" I reach for my wallet before remembering there's nothing in it except the learner's permit I got last year and a library card from a foster family three cities ago. "I'm fine. I don't need anything."

My stomach rumbles.

Evelyn studies me, then turns back to the server. "Could you add a hot cocoa and another chocolate chip cookie to my order?"

I start forward. "No, that's really not nec—"

"Sure thing," the server replies, grabbing two mugs.

I shove my hands into my pockets and stare at the floor. "You didn't have to do that."

"I know," Evelyn replies. "I wanted to. You can pick up the next one."

I mutter my thanks, too ashamed to meet her gaze.

I hate this. Hate that the vast majority of my life has depended upon the charity of others. That even now, when I'm constantly working, with barely a second in my days to rest, I am not able to pay for my own order, which comes to a whopping three dollars and fifty cents. I grit my teeth, trying to push away the anger that rises inside of me, a barely caged beast always lurking, biding its time, waiting to be unleashed again. And I hate that too. Hate that my life has created a monster within me, sticking to me like a second shadow, following me everywhere.

*That's* why I want to run away when I turn eighteen. Because maybe if I run fast enough, the monster won't be able to keep up.

A dimple appears between Evelyn's brow, and I know she senses it, the change in my mood. What must she think of me, this girl who always has her act together, who never falters, who always keeps everything moving?

I must look like a complete joke to her.

The waitress hands us our mugs and two chocolate chip cookies the size of my hands, wrapped in brown paper stamped with the Nora's logo. We grab a table by the window. I shrug off my coat, letting it fall against the back of the chair. Evelyn carefully removes hers, draping it perfectly over her own chairback.

Our mugs are each topped with a mountain of whipped cream and a candy cane. Evelyn swirls her candy cane, mixing the cream with the cocoa, then sets it neatly on a paper napkin next to her.

I haven't had cocoa since I was six. The closest I've gotten is an Irish coffee my stepdad gave me when I told him I was cold while working at his scrap yard in forty-degree weather. I didn't know it had alcohol in it—I just thought it tasted weird. I threw up my breakfast all over his work boots, and he left knuckle-shaped bruises along my jaw.

I never complained about being cold again.

Evelyn studies me over the rim of her mug as she takes a sip.

"Well, now that I've shared my own embarrassing views on existential topics," she says, "I think turnabout is fair play. So, spill."

I blink. "Spill what?"

"Your story."

"I don't have one."

"Why do I find that so hard to believe?" She leans forward, ringlets of honey-colored hair cascading over her shoulders, looking so soft that, suddenly, all I want to do is run my hands through them. "You're from Texas, right?"

My nails dig into my palms. "Yes."

"How did you end up here?"

"I came to help Uncle Bill and Aunt Bee. On the farm."

"That was nice of you."

I shrug.

"Are your parents still back there? In Texas?"

I scratch the back of my head. "My mom is. I've never met my dad. He knocked my mom up at some party. She didn't even know his last name."

"I'm sorry." She hesitates. "So...Hawthorne's your mom's last name?"

I take my first sip of cocoa to stop myself from fidgeting. It's good. Thick. Like drinking a melted chocolate bar. "Actually, a lot of people don't know this, but you can put any name you want on your child's birth certificate. It doesn't have to be the last name of either parent. Mom chose Hawthorne because *The Scarlet Letter* was her favorite book in school."

Evelyn's eyes widen. "Wow. Your mom must be really smart. That's a tough one, even for AP students."

"She just liked the message, I think. How Hawthorne pointed out the hypocrisy of the people shaming Hester Prynne for not living up to their puritanical standards even though she was a kinder and gentler soul than any of them." An image of Mom before the drugs took hold flashes through my mind, of her tucking me in at night and telling me the story in ways a small child could understand. "She named me after him as a sort of homage. She wanted it to remind me that society can be disappointing—and life even more so. But she said the most important lesson of all is that mistakes help us grow into who we're meant to be."

"That's beautiful." Evelyn sets her mug on the table. "She must be an incredible woman."

A familiar lump forms in my throat.

"What about you?" I ask.

She breaks off a piece of her cookie. "What about me?"

"Well, if you don't want to write scripts for the rest of your life, what is it that you want to do?"

She pops the piece into her mouth, clapping her hands together to dust off the crumbs. "I'm not sure. I have so many things I feel like I *could* do, it's hard to nail down anything specific. Mostly, I just want options, and I know an Ivy League school will give me those options. That's why it's so important to me that this play does well. Everyone applying has the same test scores, the same GPA, the same extracurriculars. It's almost impossible to stand out." She swallows and, not for the first time tonight, my eyes are drawn to the line of her neck. "I want to make it hard for any admissions office to reject me."

I take another sip, gently setting my mug back down on the table. "You'll get in."

"What makes you so sure?"

"Seriously? You're a force of nature, Evelyn. No one has to be around you for very long to figure that out."

"Really? Because most of the time I feel so"—she looks up at the ceiling, trying to think of the right word—"*lost*. Like I don't have any direction. When I'm in the middle of something, like the play, I know exactly what I need to do. I have steps and plans and checklists, and I feel one hundred percent certain of what I'm doing, but when I think of the future, I just—"

She swallows again.

I lean forward. "You just what?"

"I kind of wish I was already there, you know? So I wouldn't have to work so hard to figure it out anymore." She exhales. "That sounds ungrateful, doesn't it? To want to skip everything and just be there?"

"No, it doesn't," I say. "I feel exactly the same way. I just want to be...settled."

"To have a plan."

"A place."

"A purpose."

"No longer adrift."

"No longer wondering."

"To just—"

"*Be*," we both say at the same time.

We stare at each other, and it's like the room gets smaller somehow, the walls moving in and the people disappearing and the noise evaporating, so that it's just this:

Her and me.

Evelyn looks away first, tucking her hair behind her ear as she stares down at the table.

The room expands again, everything rushing back in swirls of color and sound.

"Aunt Bee swears it happens in the blink of an eye," I tell her, the chatter of families and the hum of the espresso and cocoa machines buffeting us on all sides.

Evelyn's sea-glass eyes meet mine. "Then why does it feel like every day takes a thousand years?"

"I don't know."

There's a charge in the air between us. An understanding. The feeling of being known. Heard. *Seen*. And those eyes—I could fall into those eyes forever.

I open my mouth to speak, even though I have no idea what I'm about to say. I just want to keep her here, with me, in this moment; want to unravel all that she is and all that I am and all that she makes me *want* to be. But then someone plops down loudly at the table next to ours.

Not one someone.

Four someones.

"Fancy meeting you here," Jeremy Davis says. His girlfriend Sarah sits down next to him, along with the other couple who always hangs out with them. It takes me a second to remember their names.

Evelyn leans back in her seat. "What are you guys doing here?"

"The gingerbread contest," the other guy—Graham—replies, opening his arms to gesture to the entire parlor, which has been transformed as we were talking so that every table has a tray on top of it containing the necessary items to make a gingerbread house. There are tubes of frosting and miniature bowls brimming with Skittles, M&Ms, gumdrops, lemon drops, lollipops, candy hearts, and every kind of sprinkle imaginable. Rainbow sprinkles and snowflake sprinkles and chocolate sprinkles and cinnamon sprinkles. Even glitter sprinkles.

"That's tonight?" Evelyn asks. "I can't believe I forgot."

"I can't either." Jeremy leans back in his seat. "Knowing something Evelyn Waverley doesn't? That must qualify me for some sort of record book."

Evelyn arches a brow. "To be fair, I have been a little busy lately."

"Oh yes," he says, grinning. "You two look *awfully* busy."

"It's not like that," Evelyn says, fidgeting slightly in her seat. "Beckett was helping me sort out those scenes for the second act, so I treated him to some food. That's all."

It's accurate—exactly how I would've explained our time tonight if someone had asked me.

So why is her answer so disappointing?

Jeremy looks back and forth between us, skeptical. "Uh-huh."

A server appears, bringing two trays. One for each couple.

"Are you entering the contest?" Piper asks us.

"Oh." Evelyn glances at me. "Um—"

"The prize is a basket donated from all of the locally

owned stores," Graham leans over to tell me. "The whole thing's worth five hundred bucks. Aunt Bee put in a fifty-dollar gift card, and I had to stop this one"—he gestures to Piper—"from pocketing it for herself."

Piper smacks his arm. "Not true!"

"Oh, act like it didn't cross your mind."

She sticks out her tongue, then swipes a dollop of red icing onto Graham's nose. Graham retaliates with a streak of blue across her forehead. They burst into laughter, and suddenly it's a war to see who can cover the other in more icing.

"Yes, they're wasting their resources! We've got this in the bag," Jeremy says, and then he and Sarah are debating the proper gumdrop-to-lemon-drop ratio along a proposed licorice-cobblestone path, completely forgetting Evelyn and I even exist.

Evelyn bites her lip and tilts her head in this adorable way that makes her hair swing to the side. Her eyes catch the glimmer of Christmas lights bordering the window, and I have no idea why I feel that same painful squeezing in my chest as I did earlier, but something about her makes me want to fall into her gravitational pull and never leave.

"What do you think?" she asks.

I smirk. "Five hundred bucks, huh?"

She nods.

I push up my sleeves. "Let's get to work."

# 8

## Evelyn

***

Ariana Grande's "Santa Tell Me" is playing on the overhead speakers; my friends are all laughing and sneakily sabotaging one another's houses; the air is warm and smells of hot chocolate and gingerbread while, outside, golf-ball-sized snowflakes fall like rain; and I'm trying really, *really* hard not to notice how soft Beckett's hoodie looks, or how good he smells, or how gentle his hands are as they cradle the gingerbread pieces, every bone sticking out in sharp relief as he applies just the right pressure against them so they won't break, making me wonder what it would be like to be held the same way.

Like something precious.

We spend an hour and a half on our houses, working right up until the parlor closes. Other customers left long ago, and the servers have already started placing chairs on top of tables. Each of us has had at least three cocoa refills and way too much sugar, and we sang "Jingle Bell Rock" at the top of our lungs when someone played it on the jukebox, so all of our voices are a bit scratchy.

It's one of the best nights of my life.

Out of the three houses, Jeremy and Sarah's is the best, not because they're the most artistic—Piper and Graham definitely have the edge there—but because they're so competitive. I really don't know how Sarah and Jeremy do these sorts of things without biting each other's heads off, but it's like they fuse into one person and become this power couple whenever they tackle something together. Beckett's and my house isn't bad though. We used the blue icing to make a little pond in the corner and created gumdrop people using toothpicks for legs, red hots for mouths, circle sprinkles for eyes, and licorice for hair. There are lollipop trees and white icicles hanging from the roof and even a candy cane bridge and reindeer hoof prints in the snow.

"Not bad for our first attempt," Beckett says as we all stand and take our trays over to the counter.

"I'd give the trophy to us," I say, half laughing.

"Me too," he says, so quiet I almost miss it.

I'm learning that Beckett does that a lot. Moves and speaks in small breaths, so if someone weren't paying attention, they'd miss the most important parts of him—the sacred, vulnerable parts he doles out in morsels and scraps. But the more I'm around him, the more I realize it's not in a prideful, Darcy-ish way. Instead, it's like he's guarding himself, so that if someone rejects that tiny piece, it's okay, because he kept the rest of it locked away where no one else can see.

We stare at each other, and it's like the world slows down around us. Just like the first day I met him, everything gets hazy and muffled—everything except Beckett. He stands out against the muted colors and shapes and sounds, the only clear thing my eyes can settle on.

"Whatever," Jeremy says, and like a rubber band, the

world snaps back into place. He nudges Beckett's ribs, forcing his gaze away from me. "You both know you're going down."

Beckett rubs his side, and his lips pull into a quick smirk. Then his eyes flick back to mine, and there's a question in them I don't know how to answer.

We follow Jeremy, Sarah, Piper, and Graham out onto the sidewalk and start across the snow-covered green, to the north side where our cars are parked. The snow is a good four inches deep on the grass, but the plows are keeping up with it on the streets. Still, Jeremy wonders if we'll have a snow day tomorrow, to which Graham rolls his eyes and says, "Good luck. We don't get snow days until January."

"Have faith, man," Jeremy replies. "Don't you believe in miracles?"

Graham glances at Piper, and the love in his eyes is so raw, so intense, my cheeks warm and I have to look away.

"You have no idea," Graham replies.

Beckett clears his throat and stares at the ground.

"Heads up!" Jeremy yells, decking Graham across the side of his face with a snowball.

Graham wipes the ice off his cheek. "You're a dead man, Davis."

"Only if you can catch me, Wallace," Jeremy replies.

Within seconds the snow is flying, and the couples have broken off into teams, each taking cover behind pine trees and building up their arsenal of snowballs.

I laugh at them.

Beckett shifts uncomfortably.

"I don't suppose you want to join them?" I ask him.

Snow catches in his hair and on the shoulders of his coat. His nose is already turning pink with cold. "I just...I mean...I've never—"

He clears his throat again.

My brow furrows. "You've never been in a snowball fight before?"

He shakes his head.

I smile. "It's pretty easy, you know. You just scoop up some snow"—I bend down, my fingers digging into the ice-crusted powder—"pat it in your hands like this, and—" I chuck it at his chest, the snowball splattering across his coat.

He glances down, unmoving.

I straighten my back, waiting for his reaction, my heart pounding inside my chest as my smile falters.

But then he does something I never thought I'd see him do.

He throws back his head and laughs. A *full* laugh. A howling at the moon, totally unself-conscious, from-the-diaphragm laugh, without a trace of sarcasm or cynicism or bitterness.

Just simple, pure, unadulterated joy.

"Oh, you're in for it now," he promises me, bending down and scooping up a much larger snowball.

I laugh. "What are you doing? Making a snowman?"

He keeps scooping.

"Beckett?"

He grins wolfishly up at me.

I back up, pointing my finger at him. "Now, Beckett, I want you to think about what you're doing—ack!"

I jump back, the giant snow-boulder narrowly missing me, and take off down the square, Beckett's laughter echoing behind me as our footsteps crunch the snow. I laugh too, because the snow is so thick in some drifts that our boots fall through it to mid-thigh, so that we're not running so much as jumping awkwardly away from each other while trying to gather ammunition.

I land a snowball across his face.

He flings one at my spine.

I try to duck behind a tree, but he's too fast for me, grabbing my arm and tugging me back. I lose my balance and tumble into him. He wraps his arms around me, shielding my head with his hand as I smack into the snow.

For a second, all we can do is stare at each other, our breaths coming hard and fast and uneven. Beckett's gaze trails down from my eyes to my nose to my lips and back up again.

Neither of us says a word.

"Oh yeah," Jeremy says as four pairs of feet stop next to us. "There's nothing going on between them *at all*."

"Shut up, Davis," Graham tells him. "All right, folks. Nothing to see here. Let's move it along."

He shepherds them away from us. Jeremy whistles, and they all dole out suggestive goodbyes to us as they head for Graham's car.

Beckett, looking embarrassed, pushes himself up and offers me his hand. I take it, my palm sliding across his. Two layers of gloves separate our skin, and yet the feeling of his fingers curling around my hand makes my entire arm tingle. He tugs me up, but instead of taking a step back, he stays right where he is, so that when I stand, my nose is only an inch from his chin.

He sucks in a breath.

And, for just a second, I think he might kiss me.

And I think I might—just might—let him do it.

My teeth chatter.

"You're freezing," Beckett says, taking a step back, removing the warmth his body had been radiating into mine. "Here."

He shrugs out of his coat and puts it around my shoulders.

I start to shrug it off. "I can't take this."

He puts it back on me. "I insist."

"But you'll get cold."

"I'll be fine," he says. "We're not that far from the car."

"I think you're overestimating how fast my car heats up. It *is* almost sixty years old."

He smiles again, and I decide that I like Beckett Hawthorne best when he's smiling.

"I can take it," he says. "I'm from Texas, where everything's bigger, including our ability to handle extreme weather."

I roll my eyes. "You're ridiculous."

"Not really," he says as we tromp through the snow. "You just bring it out of me."

We walk in silence to the car, him staring down at the snow, me staring at him, wondering what I'm supposed to do with this new Beckett who is not as easy to hate as the old one, and what I'm supposed to do with the fact that when he stepped away, when he didn't kiss me, I was so much more disappointed than I should have been.

# 9

## Beckett

***

I lie awake all night, reliving every moment I spent with Evelyn. Watching her mind work in the auditorium as she pored over her script; seeing the patterns and systems her brain threaded together as she spoke and wrote and spilled all of herself into finding the solution. I tried to help, but my mind faltered every time I looked at her, with that pen behind her ear and her thoughts running in circles that somehow forced themselves into perfect lines, looking so damn cute I could hardly breathe.

I relive every flutter of her lashes and every crinkle of her nose as she laughed at the slow, semi-awful progress of our gingerbread house. Relive every time she reached over me to grab a piece of candy and I breathed in her apricots-and-honey scent, a gasp of summer on a cold winter's night. Relive every time our eyes met and I lost myself in their depths, unable to form a coherent thought to save my life.

And then there was the complete joy that radiated from her entire being as we plodded through the snow. For the first time since I've known her, I watched her to-do lists and those constant thought-circles melt away. She was oblivious to the shade of pink her nose was turning, or to the way her entire body began to tremble from the cold. I kept telling myself not to give her my coat, not because I was worried about being cold, but because I was afraid it would give me away, the fact that I was noticing every little shiver, every teeth-chatter, every foggy curl of breath as it shuddered through her lips.

But not noticing Evelyn Waverley would be like not noticing a flare of light in complete and total darkness when light is all my eyes have ever craved to see.

I don't think I've ever wanted a single thing in my life more than I wanted to kiss her as I pulled her up from the snow. I almost reached for her, almost put my hand under her chin, almost tilted her lips back to meet mine, but then flashes of memories of all the times I let myself care about someone—and all the heartbreak I experienced because of it—slammed into my brain all at once. It felt like I stumbled even though I was standing still. Felt like I was falling back into a place I didn't want to be as a wall rose up between us, and suddenly, even though I knew what was coming, even though I didn't want it to, everything inside of me just—

Shut off.

And the same thought I had the day I met her came roaring back.

*No one should have that much power over any one person.*

Because that was how I'd really survived this long. It wasn't all of the charity, all of the meals provided when I was close to starvation. Those kept me going physically, but what really protected me—what really kept me safe— was deciding to detach myself from the rest of the world.

People only disappoint, and although I'm sure she would never mean to, I have a feeling that being disappointed by someone as good and kind and perfect as Evelyn Waverley would feel like being gutted by a dull blade. Too jagged, too deep, too awful to heal.

I know because it's the same way I felt the day my mother betrayed me.

That's what always gets you. The surprise attack. The one you don't see coming.

I didn't kiss Evelyn, even though I could have sworn she'd felt it too—that connection between us, that moment that seemed to stretch into eternity, when a kiss felt inevitable. But I was wrong.

I *had* to be wrong.

Because why would anyone as pure and wonderful as Evelyn Waverley *ever* want to be anywhere near someone like me?

✳✳✳

I close my locker, ready to head to rehearsal the next day, when my phone buzzes.

Mom.

I don't want to answer, but this is the tenth time she's called in two days, and even though I'm sure Serena would have told me if something was wrong, I can't ignore her any longer. I close my eyes, take a deep breath, and answer the phone.

"Yeah?"

"Honey," Mom says, her voice scratchy and low. Cogs rusted over. Nothing at all like the singsong voice I vaguely recall from my childhood, when I was too young to know it wouldn't always be this way. That I was losing her even as she stood right in front of me. "I miss you. Why haven't you been taking my calls?"

"I've been busy."

"Doing what?"

My fists clench. "What do you think?"

"*Hmm*. Careful with that temper or you'll end up just like your stepfather."

Never. I will never be like Roy.

I grit my teeth. "What do you want, Mom?"

She lets out a shaky breath. "I need money."

"And you called because...?"

"Oh, come on, sweetheart. Don't be like that."

"How do you want me to be?" I shout.

A group of freshman stare at me, unblinking.

I turn away from them and murmur, "You know I'm the wrong person to call about this. They don't exactly pay me for *community service*."

"Beckett," she says, and for a moment, I hear it, the ghost of her voice, before the drugs shot it full of holes. "I'm starving."

"So, why don't you get Roy to buy you some groceries?"

"He blew last week's paycheck at the bar."

"Like always."

She doesn't respond to that.

I stop outside the closed auditorium door. I can already hear Evelyn's muffled voice through it, calling people onstage.

"Look, Mom, you know I'd help if I could, but I can't."

"You don't have any money at all?"

"No."

"What about that money you were saving for a car?"

I turn away from the door and lean my head against the wall, closing my eyes. "We used it for the attorney fees, remember?"

"Oh. Oh yes." She says it in that way that tells me she has no clue what I'm talking about, not that I'm surprised. There are a lot of gaps in her memories. A lot of things she was physically present for but mentally checked out.

"Well," she continues, "what about Bill?"

"I'm not asking him for money—"

"And I'm not suggesting you should," she bites back. Then, softer: "He always keeps a wad of cash in his wallet. He'd never notice a few twenties missing here and there."

"Mom. No."

"Beckett, he'll never even realize—"

"*I said no.*"

There's a long, terrible pause.

"Oh. I get it." Her tone is like venom, and the echo of that dull, jagged blade twists in my gut. "You care more about what he thinks of you than what happens to your own mother. He's your family now. Is that it?"

Tears prick my eyes, and I hate her for it. "Mom, I've got to go."

"Don't you hang up on me, you ungrateful bast—"

I end the call. My eyes burn and the tears are threatening to fall, but I've done this enough times to know how to stop it. How to push away the pain. I flip the tables, telling myself she has no right to ask me for anything after all that she's done to me.

I don't let myself worry about her. I don't let myself care. I don't let myself feel the guilt or the disappointment. Anger is so much easier to handle, so I let it flood me, until every muscle in my body is as tight as a coiled spring and all I want to do is get in a fight with someone. *Anyone.*

I look at the closed auditorium door, and somewhere in the back of my mind, a voice whispers that I shouldn't go in there. Not like this. I turn to leave, but the door opens, and then Evelyn is standing in front of me, looking relieved.

"Beckett, there you are," she says. "I thought you weren't coming."

"I—"

She frowns. "You weren't leaving, were you?"

I swallow. And even though I know I shouldn't say it, my mouth forms the word "No," because I'm turning eighteen in seven weeks—fifty-two days—and the second I do, I'm leaving. I'm getting rid of my phone and hitchhiking somewhere far, far away, like I've always dreamed of doing. Somewhere no one can find me. Somewhere I can finally leave all of this behind and start over, make my own way in the world.

But I can't do that if I still have community service hours to complete.

So, even though I know I shouldn't, even though I know this can't end in any way but bad, I follow her inside, every muscle and fiber and sinew of my being crackling like a livewire, ready to take down anything and everything that gets in my way.

# 10

## Evelyn

**\* \* \***

"**W**e're doing the proposal scene," I tell Beckett. "Page sixty."
Everyone else has already been told to work on memorizing lines, and they've all huddled into small groups, so no one notices the way Beckett grits his teeth as he stalks onstage, nor how he prowls back and forth as we begin the scene, like a wolf in a cage, unable to stand still, despite the fact that his character is supposed to be the epitome of decorum and quiet reservation. His fists are clenched so tight that his knuckles are razor sharp against his skin, and the veins in his forearms stand out like ropes, barely containing the steel-hard muscle underneath.

"You know your character is supposed to be professing his love to me in this scene, right?" I ask, my heart in my throat.

Anger rolls off him in waves. "Let's just get this over with."

"Fine." I swallow. "From the top."

"In vain have I struggled," he begins, his brows slashing low over his eyes as he continues pacing. "It will not do. My feelings will not be repressed. You must allow me to tell you how ardently I admire and love you."

He doesn't look at his script once, and I would be impressed that he's already memorized his lines *if* he actually sounded like he was in love with me, but he sounds like he's about to rip out my throat.

"In such cases as this," I reply, my words trembling slightly, "it is, I believe, the established mode to express a sense of obligation for the sentiments avowed, however unequally they may be returned. It is natural that obligation should be felt, and if I could *feel* gratitude, I would now thank you. But I cannot—I have never desired your good opinion, and you have certainly bestowed it most unwillingly."

Beckett glares at me. "And this is all the reply which I am to have the honor of expecting?"

And with that, my character launches into her reasons why Darcy is the last man on earth she would ever marry. Beckett doesn't stop pacing, and I can feel his anger growing with every word. Halfway through, he starts shaking his head and laughing under his breath, a cruel sound, and I almost stumble over my lines.

"And this is your opinion of me!" he shouts as I finish, crossing the distance between us. "This is the estimation in which you hold me! I thank you for explaining it so fully."

"You could not have made me the offer of your hand in any possible way that would have tempted me to accept it," I bite back.

His muscles are so tight he's shaking, but I push the fear aside—I won't let him intimidate me. I get even closer, tilting my head in defiance.

"You have said quite enough, madam," he spits out. "I perfectly comprehend your feelings and have now only to be ashamed of what my own have been. Forgive me for having taken up so much of your time, and accept my best wishes for your health and happiness."

He's supposed to turn away from me now—supposed to "quit the room"—but he doesn't move, and he's breathing so hard his chest brushes mine with every inhale.

And then the silence in the room hits us both at the same time.

*Everyone is staring at us.*

Beckett narrows his eyes, then turns sharply on his heel and heads for the stairs.

"What the hell was that, Hawthorne?" I yell at his back.

"I believe they call it acting," he replies, not even turning to look at me.

"Hey!"

He stops halfway down the stairs.

"Get back up here," I order. "We're not done."

He turns, and I know instantly I've pushed him too far. He bounds back up the steps, coming to a stop right in front of me and bending down so that his lips are practically against my ear. His breath warms the nape of my neck, and in a voice so soft, so controlled, and yet somehow so much more powerful than when he was shouting, he whispers, "You needed a body, and I'm here. What more do you want from me?"

"I want the boy who played Darcy yesterday. The one who auditioned. The one who didn't come in here pissed off at the world and everyone in it."

His lips twist into a condescending smile. "If you don't like it, have Kyle play Darcy."

"Trust me, I'm considering it."

He laughs under his breath. "I don't need this."

He lopes down the stairs, grabs his coat and backpack in one fluid motion, and heads for the exit. I watch him go, his retreating figure doing nothing to quell my anger.

"Take five!" I yell at everyone, even though no one's doing anything except looking back and forth between me and the closing door, and then I'm storming down the stairs and up the aisle after him, practically kicking the door open on my way to the front atrium.

All the students are gone, and only every third light is on, casting dark shadows between squares of dimmed light. He's halfway to the front entrance, and even though I know he hears my shoes squeaking across the linoleum behind him, he doesn't look back.

"Hey!"

He stops, the line of his body as solid and unmovable as stone.

"I can put up with a lot of things," I shout at him, "but you choosing to be a jerk whenever you feel like it isn't one of them. Those people in there are counting on you. *I'm* counting on you."

He glances over his shoulder at me.

"If you're in," I continue, "you have to be *all* in. Either show up ready to do your part or get the hell out. I don't have room for surly prima donnas on my stage."

Beckett closes the gap between us. "Oh yeah? And do you really think Kyle can play Darcy as well as I can?"

"I would play both parts myself if I had to," I bite out through my teeth, tears of frustration burning my eyes. "It'd be better than anything *you're* giving us right now."

Before he can say anything else, I turn on my heel and stomp back inside, slamming the door closed behind me. Half of me hopes he'll race in behind me, apologize, and promise to do better. To *be* better. But the other half hopes I'll never see Beckett Hawthorne again.

I was right the first time. He's horrible and cruel and selfish. And even if the boy who made me laugh and wonder what it would be like to kiss him is still in there somewhere—even if that wasn't some strange aberration and that boy really exists—it's not enough to make up for the

fact that nine times out of ten, Beckett Hawthorne can't
be trusted.

He's the bad boy our mothers warn us about, the one who
leaves a trail of shattered hearts in his wake. I'm actually
thankful he showed up to rehearsals today ready to burn
down the world, if only so I could remember why I decided
to hate him in the first place.

## 11

*Beckett*

**\* \* \***

I storm into the courtyard, my boots punching through ice-packed snow, flipping the collar of my coat around my neck and tucking my chin down, bracing against the wind. I swear I'm heading for the farm, but when I glance up ten minutes later, I'm standing outside of Aunt Bee's bookstore. Between the fairy-lit garland framing the window and door, the lemon-yellow light pouring through the panes, and the wreath hanging from the old-fashioned gas lamp she had me hang on the brick exterior back in October, the store looks like something ripped out of the pages of *A Christmas Carol.*

She's been doing so well this year that she has an actual rotating staff now, and two guys from school I vaguely recognize are working behind the counter, taking Graham's and Piper's spots while they rehearse. I can't see Aunt Bee through the window, but I head inside anyway, a wall of solid warmth hitting me as soon as I open the door.

Tourists shuffle through the stacks, flooding out into the main walkways, their shopping bags impossible to edge around. I almost leave, but Aunt Bee pops out of her office, and I must look as terrible as I feel because one look at me and she's telling one of her employees that she's taking a thirty-minute break.

She somehow pushes her way through the sea of shoppers to stand right in front of me.

"Coffee?" Aunt Bee asks, giving me her signature, incandescent, all-is-right-with-the-world smile.

I nod.

She leads me next door to the bakery. I grimace as the smell of baking gingerbread, hot doughnuts, and sugar glaze reminds me, painfully, of Evelyn. Part of me wonders how I could go off on her like that.

The other part wonders what took so long.

We grab a table in the back. Aunt Bee waits for our coffees to be delivered, then asks, casual as can be, "What's up?"

"Nothing."

"*Something.*" She takes a sip, studying me over the rim. "You haven't looked this awful since we picked you up from the airport."

I stare at a spot on the wall, where flaking gray paint reveals the red bricks behind it. "Evelyn and I got in a fight."

"What was it about?"

I tell her everything. Well, almost everything. I don't tell her that Mom suggested I steal money from Uncle Bill, but I do tell her about the rest of the phone call and the way I acted onstage after. The way Evelyn ran out after me, and the things she said.

Aunt Bee lets out a low whistle. "She's not wrong, you know."

I twist my now-empty mug on the table. "I know."

I wait for whatever lecture is coming, but Aunt Bee just

blows out a breath and stands. "Come on. I'll give you a ride home."

I scramble to grab my things and follow her out the door. "You're not going to make me go back there and apologize?"

"You're seventeen, Beckett. I'm not in charge of your life. If you want to go back, you will. If you don't, you won't."

I narrow my eyes at her. "What's your angle?"

"No angle," she says, opening the driver's side door and sliding in as I duck into the passenger seat. "Sometimes the best thing we can do when we feel this way is to take a break, so I'm going to take you home, where you can scream or curse or take a nap, or whatever it is you think you need to do to be okay."

I wish. I've been screaming and cursing my entire life, but it's never made anything okay.

## 12

## Evelyn

***

$\mathcal{S}$omehow, we muddled through the rest of rehearsal, despite the fact that everyone kept staring at me like they expected me to self-combust at any minute, and despite the fact that, no matter how hard he tried, Kyle Caldwell could *never* be the perfect Mr. Darcy. Now everyone's packing up to go in a flurry of zippering backpacks and winter coats, whispering and laughing and darting glances my way.

Sarah and Piper stand in the aisle next to me as I gather my things. Even though I keep telling myself to forget Beckett, I'm still fuming.

"I think I have to cut him," I tell them.

"What? Like—" Sarah curls her hand into a fist and makes a *Psycho* stabbing gesture.

"No," I reply, slowly. "Like *cut him from the play*."

"You can't do that," Piper says, hitching her backpack higher on her shoulder. "I mean, Kyle's okay, but he's no Beckett."

I groan. "Why does he have to be such a *jerk*?"

"You could always follow through on your threat to play both parts," Sarah offers.

I glare at her.

"No, really," she continues, shifting her weight onto her hip. "It'd be fascinating to watch. Like experimental theater."

"Not. Helping."

Sarah rolls her eyes. "Beckett was an ass, I'll give you that. But doesn't that kind of make him the perfect Darcy? I mean, yeah, he probably shouldn't have looked like he wanted to strangle you while he told you that he loved you, but the rest of the scene was good, like he really *was* pissed off that you turned him down."

"That's not the point." I shove my pens into the front pocket of my backpack, gritting my teeth as the memory of Beckett gliding the purple one out from behind my ear, slow and smooth as silk, shoves itself into the forefront of my mind. I close the zipper on the pocket and turn toward them. "If I don't know which Beckett I'm going to get in rehearsal, then how will I know which Beckett I'm going to get on opening night? Because pissed-off Beckett is fine during the one scene that Darcy gets really angry, but other than that, Darcy is supposed to be calm. Aloof. Nothing ruffles him. Nothing gets under his skin—at least not in any obvious way." I sigh as I tug my backpack onto my shoulder. "The beauty of Darcy is that the audience gets glimpses of how he really feels in small movements, in pauses, in hesitations. Not in stalking around the stage like a predator zeroing in on its prey."

Sarah smirks. "Well, you have to admit...it *was* kind of hot."

I smack her arm. "Sarah!"

"Come on, Ev. Didn't you notice how he was staring at you?" Piper asks.

I arch a brow. "What are you two talking about?"

"Oh my gosh, it was *so* obvious." Piper crosses her arms and leans forward. "Yeah, he was pissed, but he was also pacing around like it was taking every ounce of strength he had not to push you up against a wall and kiss your brains out."

I blink. "Okay, you guys are completely delusional."

Sarah's smile widens. "Are we?"

"Yes!"

Someone clears his throat behind us.

I glance over my shoulder.

Kyle.

"Hey," he says, bouncing forward slightly on the balls of his feet.

"Hey," I say back, sounding more defeated than I mean to.

An awkward silence stretches between us. Kyle looks like he wants to say something but doesn't know where to start. Sarah and Piper glance from me to him and back again.

"We better go," Sarah says, taking a step back.

"Yeah," Piper echoes. "The guys are waiting for us. See you tomorrow."

"Bye," I say, waving vaguely in their direction, my mind still completely on Beckett and the unwelcome thought that Sarah and Piper just embedded in my brain.

Okay, the semi-unwelcome thought.

Did he really look like he wanted to kiss me?

"So..." Kyle stuffs his hands in his pockets. "How did I do?"

I force a smile. "Great. Really great."

He exhales. "That's good to hear. I was worried, you know, being the understudy. I've never been the backup before. It kind of messes with your confidence a bit." He gulps loud enough for the students heading into the front atrium to hear.

"It's strange to see you so nervous," I tell him. I've known Kyle since kindergarten. He's never been self-conscious a day in his life. "Are you sure you even want to be in the play?"

"Absolutely," he says, not missing a beat. He swallows again. "I was actually wondering if you might want to grab some food at Nora's and help me with some of my lines? My treat."

I blink. "Oh. Um—"

"I mean, I know I don't have the part officially—I know Beckett might come back—but I thought, you know, just in case he doesn't..."

The thought that Beckett might not come back should make me happy.

So why does my breath catch at Kyle's words?

I button my coat and start down the aisle, Kyle following next to me. "What part do you feel like you need help with?"

He grimaces. "All of it?"

My eyes widen.

"Not with memorizing so much," he says quickly. "But I just have a hard time understanding how exactly I'm sup-posed to be feeling as Darcy. He's kind of a complicated guy, you know?"

My eyes dart to the doors where, over two hours ago, Beckett stormed out of rehearsal. "I know."

Kyle stops. "So...can you help me?"

He looks so eager—and so helpless—I can't say no.

Besides, if Beckett doesn't come back, Kyle really is the only option we have, and maybe if I work with him enough—maybe if I can explain to him the quiet intensity that's supposed to be burning within Darcy, making all eyes find him in every crowd and every wistful heart stutter at the sight of him—maybe he can pull off something that, while not perfect, won't make me wish Beckett was the one playing Darcy instead.

**✳✳✳**

A cozy jazz version of "The Christmas Song" is playing on the overhead speakers at Nora's as we order hot cocoas and cookies. The mug is warm as the server hands it to me and the paper bag is crinkling in my hands, and all I can think about is how awful Beckett looked last night standing in this exact same spot when he realized he couldn't pay for his order. I told him he could get it the next time, but I could tell from the look on his face that he wouldn't be able to pay then either.

Is that why he was so pissed at rehearsals today? Is he having issues with money?

Kyle leads me to the exact same table Beckett and I sat in last night, and I try not to compare Kyle's bouncing, happy-go-lucky, slightly nervous energy with the weight and turmoil and mystery of Beckett's own, but it's like trying to ignore the stark contrast between the sun and the moon. And I know I should be happy to be washed in the summer glow that Kyle radiates, especially after the display Beckett put on earlier, but like the sun in a cloudless sky, the way Kyle looks at me feels like a spotlight, harsh in its attentiveness, and I miss the coolness, the hiddenness, the sheltering I feel when I'm with Beckett, and the way that the world gets kind of hazy around him, so that he's the only clear thing I see.

"So," I say, placing my coat on the back of my chair and pulling my script from my backpack. "Where should we start?"

Kyle raps his knuckles on the table. "I have a confession to make. I didn't really ask you here because of the play."

My brow furrows. "You don't need my help?"

He laughs. "You and I *both* know I do, but that's not the real reason I asked you here."

"Okay," I say, drawing out the word. "Do you need help

with pre-calc again?"

"Actually, that's another confession I have to make...I've never really needed your help in Pre-Calc. I ace every test. Numbers are kind of my thing."

I blink.

He laughs again. "Don't look so shocked. You know the dumb jock thing is just a stereotype, right?"

"No, I'm not shocked about that, I just"—I shake my head, trying to clear it—"I'm sorry, why did you ask for my help all of those times if you didn't need it?"

"Well, it's, uh..." He clears his throat. "What I'm trying to say is, I've been working up the courage to ask you something for a few months now, and I'm worried I might be too late, but I have to try—"

I break off a piece of my cookie. "Kyle, slow down."

He exhales. "Thanks." He takes a sip of his drink. Then another. Finally, he asks, all in a rush, "Do you want to go out with me sometime?"

I have no idea what I was expecting Kyle to say, but if I'd made a list, this wouldn't have even made the cut. Is he seriously asking me out? Like...*on a date*? Am I in some kind of 90's teen movie reboot where the star football player asks out the nerdiest girl in school to win a bet and nobody told me?

"I'm sorry, I must not have heard you right."

His eyes widen and he repeats himself, loud enough for the girl scouts sitting on the other end of parlor to hear. "DO YOU WANT TO GO OUT WITH ME SOMETIME?"

I pause, the cookie piece halfway to my mouth. "You mean as...friends?"

"No, I mean as...a couple."

I'm holding onto this piece of cookie so hard, the chocolate melts in my hand and crumbs fall like sand to the table. I blink away the fog curling its way into my brain and stumble over my words as I grab a napkin and wipe the chocolate off my fingers. "Kyle, that's, uh, so nice of you to ask me, but I'm super busy with school and the play, and I don't really have any plans to date."

"Anybody at all?"

"No."

"Not even Beckett?"

I hesitate. "What does he have to do with anything?"

"Nothing. I just thought, you know, maybe something was going on with you two." He clears his throat and leans forward. "Look, don't say no right away. Please. Just...think about it. I think we could have a lot of fun together."

I suddenly know how Elizabeth Bennet felt when Mr. Collins kept badgering her to marry him. But Kyle isn't a Mr. Collins. He's a nice guy, not to mention the most popular boy in school. Any girl would trip all over themselves to say yes to him. But I don't like him in *that way*, and even now, as I try to imagine myself going out on a date with him, to the movies or bowling or wherever, I can't picture my entire being falling into him the way it did with Beckett last night, and even though I want nothing to do with Beckett Hawthorne right now, I can't help feeling that, if you know how falling for someone is supposed to feel, then you shouldn't settle for anything less.

My heart is ramming in my chest and Kyle is staring at me like he's terrified I'm going to break his heart, and I'm still so mad at Beckett I could scream, and so disappointed in him I could cry, but before I can process any of it, the words, "I'll think about it," tumble from my lips.

Kyle sighs. "That's all I ask."

I clear my throat and, in the awkward silence that follows, reach for the solid ground of Jane Austen, my fingers shaking slightly as I open the script. "I do think we should work on some things for the play though. You know. In case Beckett doesn't come back."

Kyle nods and smiles as if that would be his dream come true.

And even though I thought I was stronger than this, that I could never let myself care for someone as self-centered and cruel as Beckett, that sentence echoing between us— "In case Beckett doesn't come back"—tugs at my heart and makes me wish, against my better judgment, that he hasn't left for good.

***

# 13

## Beckett

***

Thick flakes flutter like Post-It Notes outside my bedroom window from clouds grazing so low, I swear I could reach up and touch them. I try to focus on my homework, but my eyes are heavy, and fatigue is pulling at my body, willing me to sleep. I lay my head on my desk and close my eyes, thinking a five-minute doze will give me the energy I need to finish tonight's reading, but all I see is Evelyn.

I see her standing opposite me, the stage lights burnishing her hair, turning her honey-colored curls into alternating ribbons of copper and bronze. Her cheeks flushing, the line of her jaw sharpening, her entire body tensing as she stands her ground against my onslaught. It stirs something inside of me, the energy pulsing off her as we bite our words back at each other—a need to get closer to her, to meet that anger with my own, to kiss her until all of our edges turn soft.

Is it possible to melt into someone else? To consume the fire blazing in another person's eyes? I've been numb for so long I can't remember the last time I was warm. But Evelyn—

She's fire incarnate, all passion and heart and light and kindness, and I wonder what it would be like to claim that as my own. Would it help? Or would it just be another thing someone could take away? I don't think I could survive losing another thing that is precious to me, and I can already tell that a girl like Evelyn Waverley could never be anything but precious.

I wrench open my eyes, my gaze catching on the black case in my closet. My desk chair squeaks as I cross to it, running my hands over the leather, my fingers hovering over the clasps. Taking a deep breath, I do the one thing I haven't done in years.

I open it.

My violin sits inside, mahogany curves gleaming in the lamplight. It was a gift from my teacher. He knew my mom would never be able to afford one.

"I'll pay you back," I told him, already hating, at the tender age of seven, that there was nothing I could do for my mom or for myself, that everything we had was given to us. Our clothes, our thirdhand furniture, the food on our table. Even my lessons at the San Antonio Music Conservatory, the tuition of which had been collected by the staff at my elementary school after my second-grade music teacher told me I had a gift and it would be a shame to waste it.

"Just play," my teacher, Mr. Forsyth, had replied. "Give the world something beautiful. That's all I want in return."

A lump forms in my throat now as I reach for the bow.

My hand drops to my side.

I pull out my phone instead and grab the rolled-up script from the side pocket of my backpack. The number I'm looking for is on a folded-up piece of paper jammed into the front, listing the cast members along with their cell numbers and various social media handles.

*I'm sorry,* I text Evelyn. *I promise that won't happen again.*

Because she was right. People are counting on me, and I won't be the one to sink the ship.

Three dots appear immediately.

I smile in spite of myself.

*Good,* she replies. *Work on your lines. I'll see you tomorrow.*

# 14

## *Evelyn*

### ***

A heat wave rolls in overnight, shooting the high to a much more normal fifty degrees. I dodge melted slush and rippling puddles as I walk through the school parking lot, the phone conversation I had with Aunt Allison last night still ringing in my ears.

I called her at midnight. Even after Beckett's text, I was too annoyed to sleep.

"Apologizing is all well and good," I'd said, pacing back and forth in front of my dormer windows overlooking our quiet street. "But how am I supposed to trust him now? I never know which Beckett I'm going to get. He's like Dr. Jekyll and Mr. Hyde."

"Sounds more like Darcy to me." It was five a.m. in Oxford, and she had to speak over the sound of her blender as she mixed her signature green breakfast smoothie. She'd be doing yoga next, followed by a morning run and a quick shower before heading to her office in the classics and English department. "I'd be careful if I were you. We know how that worked out for Elizabeth."

"You're joking, right? After what he pulled, I wouldn't fall in love with him if he were the last man on earth."

"Something Elizabeth also said about Darcy."

I ignored her. "He's haughty, stubborn, pigheaded, a complete and *total* jerk who doesn't think about anybody but himself—"

"The lady doth protest too much."

"I DO NOT PROTEST TOO MUCH." And then I actually stomped my foot like a toddler and realized maybe she had a point.

"At least he apologized," she said after a long pause. "That's got to be worth something."

I rolled my eyes. "I'm sure Aunt Bee put him up to it."

"You never know," Allison replied. "If I've learned anything about the Darcy type, they're very rarely the jerks they're made out to be."

"Oh, what do you know?" I yelled into the receiver.

The sound of Allison's laughter echoed in my room even after I hung up.

I spot him now walking across the courtyard, wearing his signature red flannel button-up over a black T-shirt. His jeans hang low on his hips, threadbare at the knees and cutting in at his scuffed leather work boots, and I hate that I know that he'll smell like pine needles and fresh-cut tree bark, with a touch of sandalwood cologne underneath. I also hate that my breath catches at the sight of him, that my palms get sweaty and my heart races, and I can't tell if it's how angry I am at him that makes me feel so undone or something else. Something I refuse to name.

He looks up.

I force my gaze away.

Beckett walks at a diagonal until we're side by side, our

shoulders barely an inch apart, and that's another thing I hate—how aware of him I am whenever he's next to me, like the small distance between us is a wall brushing up against my skin, connecting us, so that even though we're not touching, I still feel his every move.

Beckett clears his throat. "Hey."

I side-eye him.

His lips purse into a low whistle. "Still mad. Good to know."

"Well, it was a really shitty thing you pulled."

He stops. "Wait a second."

And even though I want to keep walking, I stop too, because I was wrong. The wall is a tether. He moves, I move. He stops, I stop.

"Did I just make Evelyn Waverley swear?" he asks, incredulous.

"It's not a complete anomaly. I've been known to swear on occasion."

He laughs. "I find that very hard to believe."

I cross my arms. "What do you want, Beckett?"

"I just..." He shakes his head. "I wanted to apologize. Again."

I watch the other students filing past us, tromping through the slush. I take a step forward, lowering my voice so they won't hear. "Look, I appreciate the apology, but 'I'm sorry' doesn't make me trust you again. How am I supposed to know you won't pull the same crap in front of an actual paying audience? I need this to be the best production Christmas High has ever put on. We've already invited all of the local newspapers to review it, and I'm putting everything I have into making sure those reviews will be worth attaching to my college applications. Everyone else is working hard, doing what I ask. You're the outlier."

"I told you. It won't happen again."

"And why should I believe that?"

"Because you're counting on it." He takes another step closer, his chin ducked down into his upturned collar. He looks up at me from beneath his eyelashes—his beautiful, glorious, so-long-they-must-be-illegal-in-thirty-nine-states lashes—and I suddenly hate that about him too, the fact that something as small and insignificant as his *lashes* can make every single thought in my head turn to mush. "Yesterday was a fluke. Something happened that—" He stops. Sighs. Starts again. "It doesn't matter. The point is, I don't want you to feel like you can't trust me. The last thing I want to do is disappoint you again."

*Don't ask.* I stare into his dark caramel eyes, and I can feel the tether tightening, pulling, yanking. *Don't ask, don't ask, don't—*

"Why?" I blurt out.

"Because." He lets out a low, shuddering breath. "I—"

The warning bell rings. Beckett blinks several times, as if waking from a dream, then takes a step back, throwing up that same old wall between us.

And that action pisses me off more than it has any right to.

"Words are all well and good, *Hawthorne*," I spit out his name like it's poison. "But I won't believe it until I see it."

I turn my back on him and start for the doors.

"Then you'll see it," he says.

I glance over my shoulder.

He tucks his hands into his pockets. "Today. At rehearsal. I'll be the most dedicated actor you've ever seen."

I narrow my eyes. "DiCaprio level?"

"Please. Leo's got nothing on me."

"You know he sliced his hand open while filming *Django Unchained* and never once broke character, right?"

"Just point me to a glass I can smash, and you'll have

your very own *Pride and Prejudice* bloodbath."

A laugh bubbles up in my chest. I try to contain it, but he must see it in my eyes because he keeps going.

"I'm serious," he says, confident again as he moves toward me. "I'll smash every piece of glass on the stage if that's what you want."

"Somehow I don't think that's something Darcy would do."

"Under the right circumstances, people can be pushed to do anything."

I pause.

Silence stretches between us.

There's so much there, so much hidden behind Beckett's every word and move and gesture. What would I find if I removed every layer of armor, down to the vulnerable pieces of him hiding underneath?

I clear my throat. "See you at rehearsal, Beckett."

The right side of his mouth twitches up, revealing that dimple that makes my heart flutter. "I'll be the one smashing glasses while waxing poetic about my love for Pemberley."

And even though it's the last thing I want to do, I smile as I shake my head at him and trudge inside. A warmth spreads throughout my chest that has nothing to do with the blast of heat pouring out of the atrium's overhead vents.

*Careful, Waverley. You don't have time for a broken heart.*

And maybe I'm a glutton for punishment, but a small voice in the back of my mind echoes back: *If at least one broken heart in my lifetime is inevitable, I have a feeling Beckett Hawthorne is exactly the sort of boy I want to break it.*

# 15

## Beckett

### * * *

My phone buzzes as I close my locker, pushing textbooks and notebooks down into the muck of old crumpled-up papers at the bottom of my backpack and praying the fabric will hold. I grab my phone and hit the Answer button without checking the caller ID.

"Hello?"

I expect to hear Serena's voice—she's been on me about college applications again, reminding me constantly that it's not too late to enroll—but a familiar rattle comes over the line as my stepfather mouth-breathes into the receiver.

I know he's been on a bender even before he speaks.

"Youthinkyou'retoogoodforyourmama,boy?" He slurs, his tongue tripping all over his words.

I pinch the bridge of my nose. "What do you want, Roy?"

"I want to know why you won't send her the money."

I push my free hand into my pocket and head toward the auditorium, keeping my voice low. "I already told her. I don't have any money."

"Your mama always made sure you had food on the table. You owe her. Now take your pansy, self-righteous ass and find some."

"I'm not going to do that, Roy. So if that's all you called for—"

"It's not." He hacks up a lung into the phone. "Your mama and I have been talking, and we don't see any reason for you to keep staying there at your uncle's house. You can get just as many hours working at my scrap yard, and then you can be here to help take care of your mama."

"Isn't that your job?"

He ignores me. "Just come on home, son. It's where you belong."

Roy never calls me son unless he really needs something from me.

I laugh into the phone. "Someone quit on you, didn't they? You're short a hand. That's why you want me back. And if I'm doing it for community service, you don't even have to pay me."

"Just call your social worker and set it up. Let me know when your flight gets in."

"No."

There's a pause, like he was about to hang up but then brought the phone back to his ear. "What did you just say?"

"No," I repeat, louder this time. "You only want me there for free labor. You don't give a shit about me or my mom."

"Don't make me drive all the way out there to pick you up myself. You won't like the consequences."

"Get some coffee, Roy. Sober up."

"Listen, boy. Your mama and I *own* you until you're eighteen, which by my calculations is still more than a month away. It would be entirely within my rights to come up there and drag your sorry ass back home."

"You just keep telling yourself that, Roy."

He yells into the phone, but I'm done listening to him. I hang up and block his number.

He was right about one thing. I turn eighteen in fifty-one days. And once I do, I never have to see or speak to that prick again.

***

Evelyn's already standing onstage when I get to rehearsal, surrounded by a group of people seeking her help, as always. Everyone asks for her opinion on everything. Honestly, Mrs. Warren could use our entire rehearsal time to take naps or grade papers, and nothing would get overlooked. She's really just the supervisor; Evelyn's the one in charge, and I'd be lying if I said she wasn't absolutely mesmerizing at it.

I have no idea how any one person has that much energy, or how her brain can always be thinking three steps ahead of her and never falter. She has an answer to every question, a solution to every problem—and *organized* doesn't even begin to describe her. Just like her car, she's always perfectly put-together, not a hair out of place, not a single wrinkle in her clothes. I don't know how she does it. It's exhausting just watching her, but it's also intriguing. To see someone who has so much control, both over herself and her environment.

Maybe that's why I can't seem to stop thinking about her. Not because she smells like the best parts of summer; or because her hair shimmers in the light like threads of gold through jasper; or because, behind those sea-glass eyes, the cogs of her brain are constantly working, like she was born with this superpower where she can get three times as much done as any other human being on the planet. Not because she sometimes fixes that superpower on me, trying to figure me out, to fit me in a box, making me both furious and hopeful at the same time, because even though she's filing me away as just another project to add to her list, it means she's also thinking about me, and that has to be worth something.

No, the reason I can't stop thinking about her is because there isn't a single thing in my life I've ever had any control over, and I wonder what it must be like, to be so anchored and so driven at the same time.

I bet Evelyn Waverley has never felt out of control a day in her life.

Ten minutes into rehearsal, she calls me up onstage—and I don't know if she's trying to punish me or just making sure I can actually pull off the scene we did yesterday without being a total jerk, but she asks me to do the proposal again, and this time, when I speak, when I tell her how much I "ardently admire and love" her, I let myself really feel it, my voice softening as my mouth shapes the words in a way that sounds like a plea. *Don't reject me*, I think, even though in the book Darcy can't imagine anyone would ever reject him, especially not a woman as far below his station as Elizabeth Bennet, not when he's offering everything a woman at that time could have possibly wanted: a home, stability, financial security. Maybe I'm just inserting a piece of myself into the character, but I can't help feeling that there's a vulnerability in Darcy's proposal anyway. A deep abiding fear, because he never expected to feel this way about anyone, and to give away this much of himself feels like jumping off a cliff.

*When I give you my heart*, my very being echoes as I propose and, for a heartbeat of a moment, I don't know where Darcy ends and I begin, *don't say no.*

Evelyn sucks in a breath, and it feels like she—like *Elizabeth*—is going to say she loves me too. But of course, Elizabeth tells Darcy he is the last person on earth she would ever marry.

She shatters him.

And he responds in kind.

But this time, when I let myself feel the anger, the betrayal, the shame of her rejection, I think about how a man of Darcy's status and upbringing would react, and I channel it into a mixture of shock and controlled rage. And then the scene is over, and Evelyn is blinking up at me, a slow smile curving her pink-glossed lips that smell, even from here, like cotton candy.

"You really did memorize your lines," she whispers, amazed.

"Was I not supposed to?" I tease.

Her nose scrunches as she narrows her eyes approvingly. "All right, Hawthorne. All right."

She stares at me a second longer, then turns her back on me to call Cody, Jen, and a few others onstage, and I suddenly realize my lungs are burning.

I inhale deeply and wonder how long it's been since I last took a breath.

✳✳✳

Halfway through rehearsal, Evelyn switches gears, calling Sarah up to work with everyone on the choreography for the Netherfield ball. For the first part of the scene, the entire main cast and extras dance in a line that would've been typical of an English country dance, but then Sarah has the other couples dance offstage, into the wings, so that it appears that Darcy and Elizabeth are the only ones dancing in the room.

"The music's going to swell and you two are going to get closer, and we're basically going to be watching you both fall in love, even though neither of you really knows it at this point," Sarah tells us as everyone else heads out of the auditorium for a snack break at the cafeteria vending machines. "I'm also thinking mood lighting and maybe even a fog machine, something soft and tasteful. Thoughts?"

"Yes, to the lighting," Evelyn replies. "No to the fog machine."

"Are you sure? It could be very romantic."

I might be imagining it, but I swear Evelyn's eyes flick to me before she says, "All I can imagine is the smoke going haywire and no one being able to see us."

"Hmm, good point." Sarah looks up at the control booth and yells, "Nix the smoke machine, Jer!"

"Nixing the smoke machine!" he shouts back.

Sarah shows us the basic steps of our dance individually, and even though I'm not much of a dancer, I make sure to put some rhythm into my movements, keeping my end of the deal. I promised Evelyn I'd give it my all, and that's what I intend to do.

Sarah's eyes light up as I dance. She and Evelyn exchange a look.

"Beckett! That's amazing," Sarah squeals as I finish the final box step. "Have you ever danced before?"

"No, but I have a, uh"—I almost choke on the words—"musical background."

"Doing what?" Sarah asks.

I clear my throat. "Violin."

Evelyn looks impressed. I glance away, unable to meet her gaze.

"Well, it shows." Sarah whips her head in Evelyn's direction. "Do you think we could use that for something?"

Her brow furrows. "Maybe—"

"No."

They both stare at me.

"I don't play anymore," I tell them, shoving my hands in my pockets so they won't see them shake.

Neither of them says anything.

A beat passes.

Sarah's eyes widen. "Okay, well, I think we're ready for the real thing. Beckett."

I turn to Evelyn. Her palm slides across mine and, just like that, those old feelings stir inside of me again, the ones that long for things I can never have—*love, warmth, comfort, stability, family*—and it takes everything I have inside of me not to run in the opposite direction.

*Steady, Hawthorne,* I tell myself. *It's just a dance, and she's just a girl. You're not in danger here. No one can take anything from you that you don't choose to give them.*

My hand hovers over her hip. "Is this okay?"

Evelyn's eyes are big, round pools a guy could drown in. She nods.

I rest the curve of my palm on her hip, my thumb hooking through the belt loop of her high-waisted jeans. My pinkie rests just above her back pocket.

"Closer," Sarah says from somewhere behind me.

We each take a step toward each other, my hand guiding Evelyn forward. She looks up at me.

My throat goes dry.

And then the music starts.

# 16

## *Evelyn*

### ✱✱✱

A shiver races down my spine, all the way to my toes, every nerve ending in my body crackling as I press into Beckett. His frame is strong—even Sarah comments on how great it is—but there's a softness there too, in the way his fingers cup mine and in the way he gently pushes my hip back and forth, guiding my steps, as if I am a fragile thing and he's terrified of breaking me.

I try to concentrate, to remember which foot is supposed to go where, but every time I look up, Beckett's wolfish eyes pierce mine. He looks...timid. Uncertain. At first, I think it's just the choreography that has him acting so weird, so un-Beckett-like, but he's way more comfortable with the steps than I am. Even when I move the wrong leg, he steadies me, or when I lose the beat, he pulls me back into it.

"Are you sure you've never danced before?" I ask him, hating how breathless I sound.

He gives me a self-conscious smirk in response, and

my heart flutters again.

So, if it isn't the dance that has him so uncertain, why do his eyes curve into something soft and vulnerable and a little bit frightened every time he looks at me? Is it possible that Beckett Hawthorne, easily the toughest guy in school, is scared of *me*? I mean, I've been called intimidating before, mostly by people who didn't want to pull their weight in group projects, but this—

This is different.

Sarah stops the music. "That's great! You guys are really getting the hang of it."

Beckett lets go of me instantly, taking a step back and pushing the hair out of his eyes.

"Okay, so, I know this isn't really historically accurate," Sarah says, "but I think we should do something fancy, like a dip. Thoughts?"

Beckett stares at me, his expression completely unreadable.

"You're the expert," I tell her.

"Yes! Okay. So, Beckett is going to dip you back and then swing you around and back up, so that you'll end up pressed against him."

"Um." I shake my head, my brow furrowing. "Doesn't that feel a little too...modern?"

Sarah's entire face lights up. "But that's the beauty of it. It's hard for the audience to really *feel* two people falling in love onstage, so we need a moment, something where it feels like Darcy and Elizabeth might kiss." She gets this far-off look, like she can see the whole scene playing out in front of her eyes. "A beat will pass with you both gazing into each other's eyes, and then you'll move away from each other as the other couples slide back onstage. Then you'll both just stand there staring at each other while everyone else dances around you, really emphasizing this seismic shift that has just happened between you."

Beckett stands half turned toward me, his hands fisted at his sides, the veins on his arms bulging against his skin.

"Um, yeah," I say, forcing my gaze away from him. "Sounds good."

Sarah starts the song over. "Let's try it from the top."

Beckett swallows. His hands extend out to me, and just like at the ice cream parlor, I can't help noticing the shape of them. How strong and secure they look.

"Are you okay with this?" he asks.

Sarah rolls her eyes. "Of course she is. You're just dancing. You don't have to ask her that every time."

Beckett doesn't take his eyes off mine, waiting for my answer.

I smile. "Yes. Thank you for asking."

His palms slide across my lower back, his fingers interlocking against my spine. I draw in a breath.

"Okay, great. Now, Evelyn, you're going to bend at the knee and drop back, letting your arms swing down with your head so that your fingertips brush the floor."

Beckett's so close, I can see his pulse throbbing against the side of his neck. I bend my head back to look up at him.

"Ready?" I ask.

"I've got you," he whispers.

It takes us a couple tries to get it right. The first time, I don't lean back far enough, so I look like I'm doing some weird Hula-Hoop move rather than a graceful dip, and the second time, I lean back too far, so Beckett has to take a step forward to keep his balance.

Sarah stops us.

"Whenever you're partnering with someone," she says, repositioning Beckett's frame, "you need to think of yourselves as one person, like your bodies are connected, and you need to find your center of balance together." She takes a step back. "Try again."

Beckett's eyes lock on mine.

"Trust me," he whispers, and I don't know why I should—he hasn't exactly been the most consistent person—but for some reason, that's all it takes. The next time Sarah counts us into the dip, I bend my knees and swing back, trusting that Beckett won't let me fall. My upper body swings in a circle, my fingertips just brushing the floor, and then I'm back in Beckett's arms, my hands flat against his chest.

I look up at him, and everything slows.

His lips part. His hand reaches up, cupping the side of my face. His thumb presses against my chin, his fingers soft as feathers as they glide across my cheek. I lean forward and—

Sarah squeals.

Beckett pulls away from me so quick that I stumble forward.

"Sorry," he mutters, steadying me, and he looks like he wants to say something else but Sarah interrupts.

"That was amazing!" She does a little happy dance. "Let's do it again."

And I'm suddenly glad that everyone else is in the cafeteria right now.

# 17

## Beckett

*** 

I grit my teeth and push my nails so deep into my palms, I wouldn't be surprised if they drew blood.

Evelyn stands a foot away from me, squaring off as if we're going into battle—not dancing to a song we're supposed to be falling in love to. She stares at me like she's trying to understand what's happening between us, and I laugh because I would love to know what the hell is wrong with me right now, and why it is that no matter how hard I try to fight it, all I want to do is kiss her until neither one of us can draw breath.

The music starts and, against my better judgment, I reach for her. She hesitates, then steps into my arms, her hand in my hand, my palm against her hip, her body only inches from my own. Her shampoo wraps around me, tendrils of apricots and honey drawing me closer as we spin across the stage.

We get to the dip, and I wrap my arms around her

back. She arcs down in a perfect circle, but when she comes back up, instead of pressing against me like she's supposed to do, she pushes away from me.

I'm so caught off guard, I stumble back.

"I think that's good for today," she says, crossing her arms and staring hard at the empty first-row seats. "We really need to rehearse the Rosings Park scenes, and I know Graham and Piper had some questions about how to transition the set from Longbourn to Pemberley."

Sarah frowns. "I thought you wanted to get all of the steps mapped out today—"

But Evelyn's already heading for the cafeteria to grab everyone else, no longer listening.

Sarah shrugs at me.

I stalk down the stairs, taking my usual seat in the second row, where my backpack and green army jacket sit. I know I should be working on my lines, but my head feels fuzzy and the last thing I need right now is to read about my character falling in love with Evelyn's. I pull out my Pre-Calc homework instead and try to lose myself in the logic and consistency of numbers and formulas, where everything is simple and straightforward.

Ten minutes to six, Aunt Bee plops down into the chair next to me.

Evelyn hasn't called me back onstage once in the last hour.

I don't look up from my textbook. "You're early."

"I wanted to see how everything's coming along. Oh, just look at that set. Piper and Graham are so talented. It makes me slightly less angry with them for choosing this over the store."

"They're still working on the weekends."

She waves my comment away. "Evelyn's looking very pretty tonight."

"Whatever you're doing," I say, writing out the second-to-last equation, "stop."

She laughs.

Evelyn claps her hands together, wrapping up the Long-bourn scene she was working on. "All right, everyone. You all did great today. We'll be making our way through the third act tomorrow, so keep memorizing those lines—I don't want to see any scripts onstage next week!"

A few people grumble.

"I know, I know," Evelyn says with a little self-deprecating smirk. "I'm the worst."

Aunt Bee waits until Evelyn descends the stairs, then stands and steps into the aisle in front of her. "This is all coming along so nicely. You should be proud of yourself."

"You think so?" Evelyn glances back at the half-finished set. "It feels like there's still so much to do."

"There is," Aunt Bee agrees. "But you'll get there."

"I don't know how." Evelyn bites her bottom lip. "I would love to have a double rehearsal on Saturday, just to feel like we're getting a little ahead of schedule, but I'm working the donations booth at the toy drive that morning, and we can't even rehearse in the evening because the band needs the auditorium for their midwinter concert. I *was* able to book the auditorium for a double rehearsal on Sunday, but it still doesn't feel like enough."

Aunt Bee makes a *hmm* sound in the back of her throat. I move onto the final equation in my notebook, waiting for whatever plan Aunt Bee is cooking up in her meddling brain.

"Now, I don't want to step on any toes," she begins, "see-ing as I know how crunched you are for time, but since you can't rehearse anyway, how would you feel about inviting everyone to the farm for a little party Saturday night? We could play games and have a bonfire."

My head snaps up. Having all twenty-five students in

the cast and crew at our house for a party Saturday night sounds like the worst form of torture an introvert like myself could possibly imagine.

"A party isn't the answer to everything," I counter.

Aunt Bee arches a brow at me. "No, but sometimes all a show like this needs is a little morale boost to lift everyone's spirits." She turns back to Evelyn, laying a gentle hand on her arm. "You'd be amazed at how much cooperation you'll get from people once they've had a little break."

I stand up quickly, shoving my textbook aside. "I'm sure taking a night off is the last thing Evelyn wants to do—"

"Actually," Evelyn says, ignoring me, "I think you're right. Everyone's been working so hard. They deserve a night of fun."

"Of course they do," Aunt Bee agrees.

"I really don't think—" I sputter.

"I know! Let's make it an ugly sweater party," Aunt Bee says, as if she's just thought of this, but if I know her, that's been her plan from the start. She loves nothing more than making people dress up in humiliating outfits. "Those always seem like so much fun."

Evelyn's gaze slides to me. I mouth, "SAY NO," over Aunt Bee's shoulder.

She smirks. "I think an ugly sweater party sounds perfect."

"Wonderful!"

I glare at Evelyn.

She glares back.

Aunt Bee turns to go, then glances at Evelyn over her shoulder. "You said you're running the donations booth at the toy drive on Saturday?"

Evelyn smiles. "Third year in a row."

Aunt Bee clucks her tongue. "Those lines are always so long. Any chance you need an extra set of hands?"

"Won't you be needed at the bookstore?"

"Oh, I didn't mean me," she says. "I would love to, of course, but it is the busiest day of the year for us. No, no." She slides her gaze to me. "I was thinking Beckett could help."

I roll my eyes. Not because I don't think it's a good cause but because I'm trying to figure out when exactly Aunt Bee took charge over my *entire* life.

Evelyn arches a brow at me. "I don't think he's interested."

"Of course he's interested!" Bee leans into me a little and, with a knowing look in her eye, says, "The festival starts at eight."

And just like that, she knows she has me. If I don't help out at the charity booth, I'll lose those community service hours that would have otherwise been spent in rehearsal. But if I'm working the donations booth at eight, I can count those hours along with however much time I can get at the lot that day.

I sigh. "I'll do it."

Evelyn shakes her head. "You really don't have to—"

"I'd be happy to."

She doesn't look like she believes me, but she gives me the information anyway, telling me the booth will be on the north side of the square, directly across the street from city hall.

I wait until we get to Aunt Bee's car, then pull my phone out and text: *You agreed to that Christmas party just to spite me, didn't you?*

It feels like my heart stops, waiting for Evelyn's reply.

*You know it. ;)*

I smirk and type back: *I'm not wearing an ugly sweater. You can't make me.*

The three dots appear.

*Watch me.*

"You seem unusually chipper," Aunt Bee notices as she

pulls her car through the melting slush. "Who're you texting?"

"No one."

"Hmm." She turns out of the parking lot. "Tell Evelyn I said hi."

"Whatever you're planning, it won't work."

"Oh, darling." She laughs. "My plans *always* work."

# 18

## Evelyn

*** 

$\mathcal{S}$aturday morning dawns bright and clear, perfect weather for a Christmas festival.

Savannah and Isla are helping me set up the charity booth, stringing old-fashioned lights with giant multicolored bulbs along the edge of the table, as well as setting up a tree in the back of the white polyester tent decorated with ornaments handcrafted by the children at the hospital. Every person who chooses to sponsor a patient this Christmas gets an ornament with all of the child's information on it and a Christmas wish list, which the sponsors then use to buy presents for them and hand deliver to the hospital, where nurses place them underneath the lobby's twenty-four-foot Christmas tree. I pocket a star ornament knitted by a six-year-old girl named Amelia, my eyes quickly darting over the list she superglued to the back.

Savannah is cursing out a strand of lights that refuse to turn on and I'm positioning the lockbox that will hold the donation envelopes underneath the table when Isla sucks in a breath.

"Don't look now," she squeals, doing a perfect impression of Lydia Bennet, "but here comes your Mr. Darcy."

I glance up. Beckett is striding across the square, his hands in his pockets and the collar of his military-green coat pushed up around his ears. He has the rocker look down pat today, between his ripped black jeans, dark sunglasses, and hair pushed back into a beanie that hangs low on the back of his head.

"I wish you'd stop calling him that," I murmur, fiddling around with the lockbox even though it's perfectly tucked and secure beneath the table.

"Why?" Isla asks. "He's tall, dark, handsome, and he's got more mysteries tangled up in him than a Rubik's Cube."

"There's also his annoying cockiness and turbulent mood swings," I reply, even though I'm not entirely sure that's fair. Something seemed to be really bothering him that day he blew up in rehearsal. I just wish I knew what it was.

Savannah turns to look at him, and my cheeks warm at how obvious all three of us are, just standing here, staring. "He's objectively good looking."

Which is as close as Savannah will ever get to calling someone hot.

I groan. Apparently more loudly than I meant to because Beckett's brows arch as he approaches.

"Sounds serious," he says. "Is something wrong?" He pivots on his heel, looking back and forth at the nearly empty square. "Am I late?"

Isla giggles.

I glare at her. "No. Nothing's wrong, and you're right on time. Savannah and Isla were just leaving."

"Ah, the famous Savannah and Isla," Beckett says, taking off his sunglasses and stuffing them into his coat pocket.

He's wearing fingerless gloves that remind me, instantly, of Bender from *The Breakfast Club*, one of Isla's *many* movie crushes. Isla's eyes widen as she notices them too. Then she turns and winks at me.

I suppress another groan.

"Evelyn has told me a lot about you," Beckett continues.

Savannah crosses her arms. "She's told us a lot about you too."

He winces. "Oh boy."

"Good things, we promise," Isla says in her typical cheery voice as she puts her arm around Savannah's shoulders. "We should get going. I promised Mom we'd help set up her booth."

Savannah stares at Beckett a second longer before allowing Isla to steer her away.

Beckett scratches the back of his head. "Savannah's rather protective, isn't she?"

"She means well."

"It's a good thing," he tells me. "We should all be so lucky as to have someone like her in our lives. I'm just sorry I've given her a reason to hate me."

I'm not sure what to say to that, and my mind is too preoccupied with remembering the feeling of his hands against my spine as we danced and the warmth of his breath in my ear as I collided into him to form a coherent sentence anyway. So I just look around the square, rubbing my mittened hands together, and say, "People will be lining up soon."

"Ah yes," he says, moving into the tent. There's a space heater set up underneath the table, and Beckett sighs appreciatively at the warmth on his legs as he sits in his chair. "What exactly do you need me to do?"

I sit down next to him, my leg accidentally brushing his. I startle and fall out of my chair.

Beckett reaches for me. "Are you okay?"

What. The. Hell. Is. Wrong. With. Me?

"Yep," I say, refusing his help. "Fine."

He looks down at his hands, trying to be polite as I scramble up, but there's a ghost of a smile on his lips that sets my teeth on edge.

I slide back into my seat, careful to keep all my limbs away from his.

"It's, uh, pretty straightforward," I tell him. "All we need to do is take the donation envelopes, put them in the lockbox, and keep track of the money donated on our clipboards. Someone from the hospital will be around later to take the box. So, mostly, we just sit here."

"And write with decorative pens," he says, picking up the red pen with the giant Santa face clipped onto it.

Mine is a green pen with a reindeer.

"Exactly."

The line starts to form at eight. It's slow at first but picks up quickly. Most people make the charity booth their first stop so they won't accidentally forget to donate amid the excitement of the Christmas-themed booths and activities. Some of the booths are arts and crafts centers for younger kids while others sell everything from handmade ornaments and Christmas candies to beautiful winterscape paintings and expensive jewelry, all of them made by local artisans. There are specialty store booths and toy booths, booths selling homemade baked goods and cocoa, and booths offering knitted Afghans and wood-carved decorations. It's like walking into a Christmas wonderland.

I watch Beckett out of the corner of my eye as the festivities pick up, wondering what he thinks of it all. Wondering if the magic of holiday shoppers with their bags loaded down with presents and Bing Crosby singing "It's Beginning to Look a Lot Like Christmas" through the square's overhead speakers tugs at his heart the same way it does mine. Whether he feels transported to a winter fairyland by all the lights and sounds and cinnamon-evergreen smells. Whether he also wonders if there could possibly be a better place in the world to live.

I decide he's probably too jaded to care about anything at all, but just when I think I've got a grasp on who the real Beckett is, he does something that completely blindsides me. Like when there's a lull in the crowd an hour in and he asks me about the ornaments on the Christmas tree. There are only twenty or so left—nearly every donor has taken one. I explain about the wish lists and how the presents around the hospital's tree are always stacked five feet tall by Christmas morning.

Beckett listens quietly, then takes one of the ornaments—a T. rex wearing a Santa hat, cut out and colored by an eight-year-old boy named Justin—and stuffs it into his pocket without saying another word.

Two hours in, Savannah and Isla return.

"Mom says we should give you guys a break so you can walk around a bit and get some snacks," Isla informs us as she shoos me out of my chair.

Savannah glares at Beckett until he stands.

"How's your mom's booth doing this year?" I ask Isla.

"Incredible! We've given out so many brochures, and we've had fifteen couples already book a consultation. I have a feeling next year will be our busiest one yet."

"That's fantastic!" Isla and her mom have been working so hard to make their business a success. I love seeing it all pay off.

"We might even hire Savannah here to help out."

"No thank you," Savannah says. "I'm the last person any-one should want around on their wedding day. I'd proba-bly go on about divorce rates while helping the bride into her dress and accidentally convince her to call the whole thing off."

Isla blinks. "Or you could also just...not."

"Sorry, but I don't think that's an option."

Isla rolls her eyes. "Girl, we have *got* to get you a boyfriend."

They're still bickering as Beckett follows me out of the tent and onto the cobblestone path, lined in mud from the melted snow. "Be back in twenty," I call over my shoulder, but neither one of them is listening to me.

I laugh and shake my head.

"Savannah is...intense," Beckett says.

"She's really very kind and good natured. She just doesn't do the whole 'love' thing."

"Sounds like there's a story there."

"There is," I say. "Mostly, there's just been a lot of heart-break in her family, and I think Savannah believes she can avoid it if she can categorize love as a choice people make as opposed to something that happens to them."

"What do you think?"

Beckett's eyes are as dark and warm as cups of freshly brewed coffee, and for a second, I can't breathe. "Huh?"

This boy makes me dizzy.

"Is it a choice?" he says, quietly. "Or something that happens to you?"

"I...don't really know. I've never been in love."

"Me neither."

We both stare hard at the ground as we tromp over to Nora's booth. I grab a mug of hot cocoa and offer to buy Beckett one also, but he refuses. I want to ask him why he never has any money on him, considering all the work he's been doing at the tree lot, but I don't want to be rude, so instead, I say, "I didn't know you played violin," thinking of our conversation yesterday.

"Not many people do."

"How long did you play?"

"Three years. From seven to ten."

"How did you get into it?" I ask. "Did your mom play?"

He shakes his head. "My second-grade music teacher thought I was good enough to learn from one of the professors at the San Antonio Music Conservatory. That's where we lived then. San Antonio." He kicks at a loose pebble on the walkway. "I even gave a performance there. At the conservatory."

My eyes widen. "Wow. You must be really good."

He shrugs.

"Why did you stop playing?"

"It's complicated."

"Oh."

A beat passes.

He sighs. "My mom owed people some money. Not very nice people. We had to skip town. Made our way to Boulder for a while and crashed on her friend's couch. I tried to keep up with it, but we didn't have money for lessons—my conservatory lessons were all funded by the staff at my elementary school—and we didn't stay in one town long enough to find a good teacher anyway. I, uh"—he clears his throat—"I had kind of a rough childhood. I don't really like to talk about it."

"Then we won't talk about it."

He swallows. "Thanks."

We pass by a booth selling roasted chestnuts, and this time I insist on buying some for us to share. Beckett says he's never had any, and I tell him it's my duty as a Christmas, Virginia resident and all-around Christmas lover to rectify that. The vendor scoops up a giant helping into a newspaper funnel and hands it to me. I give him three dollars, take a handful, and then pass the funnel to Beckett.

He takes a bite and makes a horrible face. "These taste like mushy cardboard."

I laugh.

"Seriously." He chokes. "How can you eat these?"

"You get used to them."

He shakes his head at the funnel. "How did this ever become a holiday tradition?"

"Same way stringing popcorn on a tree and eating those little chocolates in the Advent calendars did, I suppose."

"Yes, but those are both delicious." He hands the chestnuts back to me. "These are an abomination."

"Don't let anyone else in this town hear you say that. They might kick you out."

He laughs. "Noted."

We start down the length of the east side of the square, heading toward city hall, where a small ice rink has been erected and carriage rides pulled by snow-white Clydesdales are offered for two dollars a ride, all proceeds also going to the children's hospital. I almost ask Beckett if he wants one but sharing a blanket on a cozy red velvet carriage seat built for two feels way too suggestive, especially considering what happened during yesterday's rehearsal.

Sarah was pissed we didn't finish choreographing the ballroom scene, and she's been texting me about it all morning. And it's a big moment, I know—the moment the audience sees Elizabeth and Darcy falling in love—but every time I think of stepping into Beckett's arms again my heart starts flipping around in my chest like an Olympic gymnast and my palms get all sweaty and my mind goes completely blank.

How we're going to pull it off on opening night is beyond me.

I'm so lost in my thoughts it takes me a moment to realize Beckett isn't walking next to me anymore. I stop and glance over my shoulder. He's staring at the classic cars lining this side of the square, all decked out for the holidays with wreaths on the front grilles and twinkle lights framing the windows.

"Want to check them out?" I ask.

He glances at me, an unfamiliar light shining in his eyes. "Do we have time?"

I nod.

He smiles, then moves toward a vintage red truck with rounded bumpers and a Christmas tree tied up in the bed. The owner tells us it's a '54 Chevy, and my heart aches, thinking of my grandpa. He always loved looking at old cars.

Beckett runs his hands over each of the cars we see, just like he did with mine. He asks the owners questions about maintenance and finding historically accurate parts. He is so engrossed in the cars—and I am so engrossed in watching him—that I forget to check the time until Isla texts me.

*How's it going? ;)*

I glance at the clock. We've been gone for thirty minutes.

*Crap*, I text back. *I'm sorry. Be there in two seconds.*

*GIRL, TAKE YOUR TIME*, she replies. *It's not every day you get to walk through a magical Christmas festival with your soul mate.*

**Me:** *He's not my soul mate.*

**Isla:** *You just keep telling yourself that.*

**Me:** *We'll be back in five minutes, tops.*

**Isla:** *Engaged, I hope.*

And then she sends a GIF of Beyonce sassily pointing to her left ring finger.

**Me:** *Tell Savannah to smack some brain cells back into your head.*

**Isla:** *Love you tooooooo. <kissy-face emoji>*

I roll my eyes and stuff my phone back into my pocket, then move next to Beckett. He's staring at a navy-blue two-door that has the rounded curves and circular headlights of the fifties and the smooth finish indicative of more luxurious brands.

"This is my future car," he says, breathless.

"What is it?"

"A 1953 Aston Martin DB2."

"It's incredible," I tell him, taking in the sleek lines and soft leather interior.

"Expensive too," the owner says gruffly, frowning at Beckett's ripped jeans and the bar in his ear. "Need a good job to pay for one of these."

"I don't doubt it, sir," Beckett replies, so much more polite than I think I would be if someone spoke down to me like that.

The man clucks his tongue against the roof of his mouth. He's wearing a vintage leather Aston Martin jacket, his silver hair thin on top and long in the back. I don't recognize him—he must have driven the car in from another town.

"What kind of job do you think you can get wearing clothes like those?" he asks, turning back and laughing to a 50-something-year-old woman with fake blonde hair and even faker lips.

Beckett opens his mouth, but I lay my hand on his arm, stopping him.

"Whatever he does with his life," I tell the man, "at least I know he won't turn into an asshole like you."

The man narrows his eyes. "You can't talk to me like that."

Beckett rubs his hand over his mouth, hiding his grin. "I believe she just did." He puts his arm around my shoulders, holding me tight against his side. It's both an intimate gesture and a protective one. "Have a good day, sir."

And with that, Beckett leads me away from the classic cars, toward the gazebo in the middle of the square. I think about the last time we were here together. Snow flying. Beckett's body on top of mine. Pulling me up against him. Our breaths shallow. The very air around us charged with expectancy.

And here I am again, pressed up against his side, his arm draped over my shoulders, his hand hanging limp and careless in front of me, as if this were the most natural thing in the world for him to do. And it feels that way. Natural. Like we were always meant to be like this.

Beckett waits until we're a good distance away from the old man, who's gesturing at us and shouting profanities, before letting me go and stuffing his hands back into his pockets.

He clears his throat. "Thanks."

I cross my arms over my chest, suddenly cold from the absence of him. "He had it coming."

"Still, you didn't have to do that."

I stop. "Yes. I did."

He stares at me a moment. Opens his mouth. Closes it.

I smile at him, an unspoken understanding hovering in the air between us, and then we start back toward the booth. It looks like it slowed down after the initial rush, but there's always a second wave closer to lunchtime.

"Why do you love old cars so much?" I ask as we walk.

"One of my foster families"—he pauses, his eyes cutting to mine, judging my reaction; I keep my face blank, even though my heart tugs painfully at the way his voice cracks on the word *foster*—"took me to a car show once. I'd already spent most of my life thinking about running away, but before that car show, I pictured myself hopping a train like some sort of 1920's orphan. But the car show—" He exhales. "That was the first time I knew a car could be a work of art, not just something that helps you get from point *A* to point *B*, and I was consumed by the idea that, someday, I could get in something that beautiful and just drive and drive and drive, until I ended up somewhere no one knew me. Somewhere I could start over." He shakes his head. "It's foolish, I know. I'll never be able to afford one off of part-time jobs, even if I could manage to stay in one place long enough to get any sort of consistent paycheck. It was dumb thirteen-year-old logic, I guess."

"It's not dumb," I tell him. "It's poetic."

He shrugs. "Now, when I imagine running away, I'm back on that train or in some beater I'll be able to afford once I sell my violin."

"You want to do that?"

"What?"

*Run away?*

I swallow. "Sell your violin?"

"I don't use it anymore."

"That's not what I asked."

His jaw ticks. "I'll have to do something. I can't stay here."

And there it is. The reason I can't fall for Beckett Hawthorne. Because no matter what happens between us, he's transient, a vapor, here one day and gone the next, and if books have taught me anything, it's that it never works out well for the girl who falls in love with a ghost.

# 19

## Beckett

### ✳✳✳

efore Aunt Bee invited the cast over for a party just to spite me, the only Christmas decoration to be found in the entire farmhouse was a lone Christmas tree framed in the front window (and that was only because Aunt Bee said it didn't look good for the owner of a Christmas tree farm to not have his very own tinsel-laden pine in view of the interstate), but when I come down the stairs at ten-to-six Saturday night, throwing on a fresh Henley and pushing my hair out of my face, it looks like Santa's elves spent the entire day turning the first floor into a North Pole replica.

Evergreen garlands with giant red bows and dangling boughs of holly frame every doorway. The kitchen table is covered in a white lace tablecloth with sparkly poinsettias stitched along the edges, and the sugar-butter smell of freshly baked cookies wafts through the air, riding the jazzy notes of an instrumental Christmas playlist. There's hot cocoa and cinnamon apple cider on the stove and

Christmas-themed mugs all lined up in rows.

And every single room now has its very own Christmas tree.

The kitchen has a baby pine sitting at the table as a centerpiece, decorated with tiny tinsel and a little star on top. The dining room has a tall, spindly one in each corner, all four of them decorated in ribbons and ornaments of scarlet and gold. The front room tree is still the same, decorated with family ornaments—mostly retro ones from Aunt Bee's and Uncle Bill's childhoods in the '40s, their high school and college years in the '50s, and their brief marriage in the '60s—a time Aunt Bee has only talked to me about in fits and spurts (mostly about how they just weren't growing together in the way a married couple should) but that I can never get Uncle Bill to shed a single light on.

There's also a real, wood-burning fire in the fireplace and stockings hanging from the mantel, where a little porcelain Christmas village sits atop a bed of wispy cotton balls that have been stretched out to look like snow, and just like at the festival today—when I couldn't help but wonder what it would have been like to have grown up in a world where people had the money to buy unique Christmas presents for their loved ones and take horse-drawn carriage rides through the snow and even eat those disgusting roasted chestnuts just because it was the thing to do this time of year—somewhere deep inside my chest, something starts to ache.

Footsteps thump up the cellar steps, and I hear Bill's low, muffled voice say something that makes Aunt Bee laugh.

"Well, I appreciate it," Aunt Bee says, her voice getting louder as they make their way toward the first-floor landing. "It wouldn't be a real Christmas party if we didn't have this displayed front and center."

"Do you remember where we got it?" Bill asks her.

"How could I forget?"

There's barely an inch of space between them on the landing, and it feels like a private moment, one I shouldn't be watching, but the floor is old and creaks with every step, and I know if I move, I'll interrupt whatever they're sharing. And for some reason, it feels really important that I don't. So I stand still, my hands in my pockets, waiting for them to notice me.

"Salzburg," Bill whispers.

"Our honeymoon." There's a weight to Aunt Bee's smile, a distant heartache getting drudged up along with the memory.

Bill edges closer. "The Christmas market was unlike anything I'd ever seen."

"Me too."

"Do you remember the choir?"

"And the candlelight?"

"The pastries?"

"The cheese?"

They both chuckle.

Bill lowers his voice. "The saxophone player?"

"You took me by the hand and danced with me as the snow fell down around us." She lets out a breathy exhale, and even from here I can see the tears brimming in her eyes. Uncle Bill slowly, hesitantly, places his hand on her arm, and Aunt Bee leans into him, pressing her forehead against his.

The moment stretches on. I don't want to interrupt, but the cast is going to be here any minute and I don't want it to look like I've been spying on them.

I clear my throat.

They both look up.

"Ah, Beckett," Aunt Bee says, wiping the tears from her eyes and laughing at herself. "Look what we found!"

She holds up a wooden clock that looks like an old-world cottage, with snow on the roofline, garland around the balcony, and painted candles in the windows.

"Cool," I say.

"Wait for it." She winds the clock, and as it strikes six, the little doors on the balcony open and Santa's sleigh—complete with eight tiny reindeer; a red velvet bag full of toys; and the jolly, bearded man himself—slides out.

"A cuckoo clock," I say.

"A *Christmas* cuckoo clock," Bill adds, coming to a stop next to Bee. "From Austria."

"I didn't know you guys went to Austria."

"We did an entire European tour. England, France, Italy, Austria," Bee says. "We had a very small, very inexpensive wedding, so my parents offered to pay for the plane tickets and train fare. All we had to pay for was the food and lodging."

"It was the best two weeks of my life," Bill says.

Bee smiles. "Mine too."

They stare at each other.

I stare at the floor.

Bee exhales suddenly, as if waking from a dream, and holds up the clock. "Well, where should we put it?"

And then they're off, circling the room, trying to find the perfect spot.

I head into the kitchen to grab a water bottle, giving them their space. For two people who supposedly made each other so unhappy, they share a lot of hushed, quiet moments together, reminiscing about a time when they didn't sound unhappy at all.

Bee walks in a minute later, her eyes widening as she takes in the absence of a single ugly holiday design on my shirt. "Oh no. You're not wearing that."

I glance down at myself. "Pretty sure I am."

She rolls her eyes, disappears into the family room, and comes back with a dark-green sweater with a giant reindeer face on it and a red sparkly ball on the nose. "This is for you."

"I don't think so."

"Where's your Christmas spirit?"

"I lost it in all the decorations."

She zeroes in on my water bottle. "And you're not drinking that."

"Again, pretty sure I am."

"There's nothing festive about water."

"And there's nothing festive about diabetes either."

She crosses to the crockpots, grabs a mug that looks like a giant Santa face, and pours warm apple cider into it before taking the bottle from my hand.

"If you're not going to wear the sweater, at least drink the cider."

I laugh. "Yes, ma'am."

The doorbell rings and she starts for the door, then turns back to me, her finger wagging. "I'm going to get you in that sweater before the night is through."

"Don't count on it."

"You'll succumb to the peer pressure."

"I never have before."

"Or maybe it'll just take a certain *someone* to get you in it." Aunt Bee arches a brow. "Evelyn Waverley perhaps?"

"There's not a person on earth who could force me into that monstrosity."

Aunt Bee makes a *hmmph* sound and heads for the door. I lean back against the kitchen cabinets and try to look like I'd rather be anywhere than here, which is true—a party is literally the stuff of my nightmares—but, for some reason, my heart flips over like a flapjack, hoping Evelyn will be the first one through the door.

And of course, true to Evelyn Waverley form, she is.

"Right on time," Aunt Bee says, giving her a hug and taking her coat. "We've got cocoa, cider, and cookies in the kitchen. Help yourself."

Evelyn's ugly sweater—pink with a pattern of white silhouetted reindeer, snowflakes, and angels—is way more adorable than it has any right to be.

"I don't think that sweater qualifies as ugly," I tell her.

She grins as she walks toward me. "Neither does yours. And at least mine's a sweater."

"Touché."

"I heard there are cookies around here somewhere?"

"Follow me."

Evelyn's boots click across the old farmhouse planks as I show her into the kitchen. She grabs a snowman mug and chooses the hot cocoa, sprinkling mini-marshmallows on top. She also procures a cookie, stuffing it into a little napkin envelope, perfectly encased so as not to shed a single crumb onto the floor.

She points to the Rudolph sweater. "Is that yours?"

"Supposed to be."

"Too cool to wear an ugly sweater?"

"Someone has to look out for my street cred. Aunt Bee's clearly not going to."

"You do realize this is supposed to be a team-building exercise, right? How will it look if one of the play's central characters refuses to participate?"

"Actually, it's supposed to be a party." I lean forward, my hands in my pockets. "Not everything's about productivity, Ms. Waverley."

"In my life it is, Mr. Hawthorne."

"Then maybe you need to have a little more fun."

"Says the guy who refuses to wear an ugly sweater to an ugly sweater party."

"You want me to wear the sweater?"

She nods.

I pull the sweater off the chair and put it on.

Evelyn laughs, and that ache I felt earlier intensifies.

"Perfect," she says, staring up at me with her twinkling sea-glass eyes.

We stare at each other for a second too long, and I wonder if she can hear how fast my heart is beating, because something about Evelyn shifted for me at that festival. I think it was something in the way she didn't push to hear more of my story, or in the way she defended me to that creep. I've been defending myself against people like him for so long, it's become second nature to just politely respond and move on, but Evelyn cared enough to put him in his place, and that meant more to me than a thousand Aston Martins.

This whole time, I've been attracted to Evelyn, to her ability to handle whatever comes her way. To her smile and her confidence and her sea-glass eyes. But everything feels deeper now. More significant. And I'm not sure what to do with all of these feelings when I'm leaving in less than two months, and the future I've planned for myself does not include pining away for a girl in Christmas, Virginia who is definitely much too good and kind and lovely for someone like me.

The doorbell rings again, and it sounds like a group has arrived as several voices shout how "awesome" the decorations look. Evelyn smiles at me, and I feel it in that moment like I've never felt it before—the way my soul is tying itself to hers—and I know whatever comes next will either shatter me or remake me, and I'm not sure which would be better.

I can't imagine leaving her.

And I can't imagine staying.

Therein lies the problem.

And as Evelyn makes her way back to the front room to greet everyone, she is completely unaware of the fact that she's taking another piece of me with her that I didn't mean to give away.

# 20

## Evelyn

### ***

Aunt Bee was right. The cast needed this.

They needed cocoa and cookies by a roaring fireplace; needed charades and Pictionary and freeze-dancing to Michael Bublé Christmas music; needed a night off from memorizing and rehearsing; needed a second to breathe, to live. To not think about anything past this moment, this night.

I probably needed it too, but the anxiety's already creeping in, making my chest tight—that old, familiar feeling that there's more that I could and *should* be doing with this time. That by taking a night off, I'm actually just creating more work for myself tomorrow. And sometimes I swear no one else views time like I do, like every second is a coin and each person only gets so many of them in their lifetime. When the time comes, when my coins run out, I want to be able to look back and know I spent them well.

It's easy to know if they're spent well on tangible things, but it's so much more confusing on a night like this. Is a coin spent well in laughter? Or in jumping around, waiting for the music to stop so you can freeze at just the right moment? Is this just as important as the boxes getting checked off of my endless to-do lists? I'm not sure, but one thing I do know:

I haven't been able to stop staring at Beckett Hawthorne all night.

At his hands and his long, thin fingers; at the curve of his knuckles and the outline of his bones; at the soft, blue swell of his veins, rippling like rivers up his wrists; and suddenly I want to trace them, to sketch the tattoo peeking out from the cuff of his shirt, to feel the softness of his skin and the hardness of his frame beneath my fingertips. And then, just as suddenly, I want his hands to trace me, to feel that electric shock again, the way he immobilizes me, pinning me in place whenever he touches me.

I stare at his hair, at the way it falls into his eyes every few minutes before he pushes it back. At the way he leans against doorframes, his arms crossed, making the curl of his biceps push against his sweater. And I hate that I'm so aware of him, this boy who will walk away from me and never look back. Because I don't know if Beckett has been feeling the same tug toward me that I have toward him, the same tether that inextricably binds us, pulling us into each other whenever we occupy the same space, but however he feels about me, he's made it *very* clear I'm not enough to make him stay.

Staring at Beckett Hawthorne is dangerous.

So, why can't I look away?

He's so far managed to avoid joining in on the festivities, and I imagine if it were up to him, he'd be up in his room right now, drowning out the party with loud, thrashing rock music and reading a book by an equally dark, jaded author. Vonnegut, maybe, or Kerouac. But sometimes— *sometimes*—as he watches us act out movie titles on strips of paper or draw stick figures on the white board Aunt Bee pulled out for Pictionary, he gets this look in his eyes. A longing, starving look, like he wonders what it would be like to be as carefree as the rest of us.

I recognize it because it's the same look I must give off whenever I glance around at my cast and crew—my friends—and wonder if they, too, are feeling the anxiety of knowing there are still things to be done, or if they are as fully invested in the present moment as they seem.

I glance at Beckett again and, not for the first time, catch him staring back, and I know he sees it too. The same question in my eyes.

What would it be like to *really* have fun?

"All right, kids," Aunt Bee says, appearing in the doorway next to Beckett, bumping him with the corner of a large white box with red, blue, yellow, and green circles on the side. "Bill's setting up the bonfire, which means we have time for one more game before making our s'mores."

Beckett's eyes widen as he takes in the game. Twister. He starts backing out of the room. "I think I'll just go help Uncle Bill—"

"Nonsense," Aunt Bee says, nudging him forward. "You haven't played a single game tonight. Who wants to see Mr. Darcy perform daring acts of flexibility?"

The whole cast cheers. Well, almost the whole cast. Kyle just stares at him, a muscle in his jaw ticking.

Beckett shoves his hands into his pockets.

"Perfect." Aunt Bee claps Beckett on the back. "And whom else shall we nominate to pretzel themselves for our enjoyment? Your illustrious director, perhaps?"

Everyone claps and shouts my name, except for Kyle, who goes white as a sheet.

A weight presses against my chest as I meet Kyle's pained gaze. I still haven't given him an answer, and I know I have to—I know letting him think that there's hope for us when I can't stop staring at Beckett is cruel—but there's this small, defiant part of me that's screaming that Kyle is the type of boy I *should* be dating (safe, steady, reliable Kyle), *not* Beckett, and that voice makes me want to say yes to Kyle and completely forget Beckett Hawthorne ever blew into our sleepy, Christmas-obsessed town in the first place.

But then Beckett does something ridiculous—like push his hair out of his eyes; or shove his sleeves up to his elbow; or stare at me like I'm the moon and he's the tide, being swept into something beyond his control—and I'm mesmerized by him again.

What is wrong with me?

Aunt Bee pushes me into the middle of the room, and I forget all about Kyle as I take in the fact that I'm about to play Twister with Beckett Hawthorne in front of my entire cast. How *exactly* am I supposed to bend my body around his when the simple act of his palm sliding across my own makes me lose every bit of common sense in my body?

"I think I'll sit this one out," I start to say, taking a step back, but the others boo and push me forward again.

Aunt Bee nominates her employees, Graham and Piper, to join us, which is so not fair because they certainly won't be embarrassed if they get all tangled up in each other. But Beckett and I—

I push the thought away.

While Piper and Graham help Aunt Bee lay the Twister map on the floor, Beckett slides next to me, barely containing his laughter.

I narrow my eyes at him. "What are you so happy about? You have to do this too, you know."

"I know, but seeing you endure the same torture is taking the edge off."

I bump him with my shoulder. His lips pull into a smile,

and my heart feels like it might burst right out of my chest.

Jeremy decides to be the spinner, sitting in the over-stuffed chair next to the fireplace and calling out our positions. It starts innocently enough. Graham and Piper both have a foot on red. Beckett places a hand on green. And I'm thankful to get a foot on blue.

If I could get "feet" the entire time and never have to bend over, that would be ideal.

Too bad the statistical likelihood of that happening is extremely low, and a few more spins in, not only am I bent over, but I'm making a bridge over Beckett, who is crouched underneath me in the crab-walking position. Graham's and Piper's legs are tangled, and Graham's forehead is pressed against Beckett's jaw.

Piper is the first one out since she's not tall enough to keep her foot on green *and* place her hand on the only available red circle. Graham follows two spins later, when he tries to twist his body like a corkscrew to get a hand on the blue underneath me. He falls and almost takes me with him. I think about pretending to fall anyway to make it stop, but I'm too much of a perfectionist to do that. Even when I don't want to play a game, my competitive nature kicks in and I refuse to settle for anything less than first place. So when Jeremy calls out right hand yellow, I twist my body into a crab position on top of Beckett's own and—

END UP WITH MY BUTT DIRECTLY ON TOP OF BECKETT'S CROTCH.

I startle and pitch forward, just barely saving myself.

Everyone else is laughing, and all I can think is: *I AM MIDAIR SPOONING WITH BECKETT HAWTHORNE IN FRONT OF OUR ENTIRE CAST. AND THEY'RE ALL TAKING PICTURES.*

There's no way this visual isn't making its way onto the phones of every Christmas, Virginia resident by midnight.

My cheeks are a thousand degrees, and I'm trying not to focus on the warmth of Beckett's breath fanning across my ear, or on the way his breath seems to wobble slightly, like this is just as uncomfortable for him as it is for me.

Jeremy's laughing so hard, he can't spin.

"Jer," I grit out through my teeth.

He sucks in a breath.

"Jeremy."

He throws back his head and laughs harder.

"JEREMY DAVIS, IF YOU DON'T FLICK THAT SPINNER—"

"I got it, I got it," he says, wiping away tears. "Beckett, left foot red."

Beckett grunts slightly as he shifts his weight, swinging over top of me to place his foot on red, and I suck in a breath. Because now we aren't spooning—now he's hovering over top of me, the zipper of his jeans not even half an inch away from my own, and I am engulfed in the broadness of his shoulders, his eyes, his nose, his lips, our bodies millimeters from touching.

The sounds of everyone laughing falls away, along with the Christmas music and the roar of the fireplace. Jeremy calls out that I'm supposed to twist my body around to place my right hand on green, and I'm so caught up in the sound of Beckett's breathing and in the way his eyes keep trailing my lips that it just barely registers. I move slowly as Beckett arches his back to give me room to maneuver, and it's like a dance, the way we arch and slide and move around each other. I place my right hand on green. My spine presses against his stomach. His cheek, just beginning to roughen with stubble, scratches my neck, and I have never been more aware of another human being in my entire life.

Seconds pass like minutes, and still, it is too short, because a spin later, Jeremy asks Beckett to make an impossible move. He topples onto me, and we both fall onto the mat.

Everyone cheers and claps and declares me the winner, totally unaware that my heart is racing and my head is spinning, and if someone asked me right now, I don't know that I'd be able to tell up from down.

My eyes lock on Kyle, and suddenly, it's obvious.

He knows how I feel about Beckett.

Aunt Bee yells from the back door that the bonfire is ready and everyone should come claim their sticks for s'mores. Kyle shuffles out behind everyone else, his head down, hands in his pockets and his shoulders drooping, and suddenly it's just me and Beckett left alone in the room together.

Still tangled up in each other.

Still breathing as if we've just run a marathon.

His lips tug into a half smile. "Hi."

My own smile mirrors his. "Hi."

He swallows. "We should, uh, probably head outside."

Am I imagining the roughness in his voice?

He clears his throat, and I know I'm not.

"Yeah," I say. "We should."

He gets up first, then reaches out a hand to help me. My palm slides across his, and we both suck in a breath. I let go as soon as I'm on my feet and start for the kitchen, where everyone else has already disappeared out the back door.

"Evelyn?"

I stop.

He sidles up to me, all swagger and easy confidence.

"For the record," he says, "sharing you with everyone else is the *last* thing I want to do right now."

He moves past me, out the door, and I'm standing there, completely frozen.

Because I can feel myself falling for Beckett Hawthorne.

Because I'm pretty sure I fell for him the first day we met and every day since.

Because falling for a boy who will, undoubtedly, break my heart is going to derail everything I thought my senior year was going to be.

And yet I can't seem to stop.

It isn't until I'm out by the fire and Beckett hands me a stick with a marshmallow already pierced through it that I realize when I'm with him, the anxiety fades. The to-do list disappears.

It is just him.

It is just me.

And the magic inherent in that feels so thin, so fragile, that I'm suddenly terrified to even breathe for fear the spell will be broken.

For the first time in a long time, I'm present.

I'm having fun.

# 21

## Beckett

\*\*\*

The bonfire, set up in the large yard between the house and the cornfields lying fallow for the winter, reaches for the night sky, stretching black and cold above us. The stars are out, and the nearly full moon shines down its silver-blue light on the frosted grass. Everyone is huddled together in their winter coats and hats, warming themselves by the flames while marshmallows turn golden brown and gooey on sticks, and foggy clouds of snow-white breath tangle in the rising smoke as the entire cast jokes and laughs and sings Christmas songs like a pack of wild animals.

But it is not the fire that warms me. Not the mass of us all huddled together.

It's her.

Only and completely her.

I've spent the entire evening watching Evelyn Waverley. Watching the way she fidgets, trying not to check the time on her phone, her foot bouncing midair when she sits with her legs crossed or gently rocking back and forth on her heels when she stands. The way she can so easily offer a kind or reassuring word to someone or engage in a conversation with a sparkle in her eyes, as if she had been with them the entire time and not a million miles away, her mind churning and her fingers itching to reach for those multicolored pens.

Evelyn Waverly is a girl on a mission. She never stops, never rests. I imagine even her dreams contain lists to be checked off and ideas for new projects. But I saw it all fall off of her, like a curtain dropping to her feet, the second I stood next to her for that game that I used to hate, and maybe it makes me the worst sort of pretentious, self-centered egomaniac to think that I might have an effect on her that others don't, that I can somehow pull her out of herself so she can just *be*, or maybe it is only wishful thinking, that I might have something of value to offer her—that I might be worthy of her—but whatever it is, she is different around me. And that gives me hope.

She chooses to stand next to me by the fire. Chooses to share a bag of marshmallows with me. These are all her friends—she could have chosen to do the same with any one of them—so the fact that she is standing here, so close I can smell apricots and honey just as strongly as the flames and the pines, makes me bold. Makes me into a person I think I may have once been—or would have been, had my life run a different course. Either way, she makes me *more*. More daring. More mischievous. More willing to jump. To give those pieces of myself. To trust again.

More.

More.

More.

That's all I want.

More of her.

More of me.

More of us and whatever it is we're becoming when we're together.

So, when everyone shouts like a pack of hyenas for another game and someone suggests hide-and-seek, I reach for Evelyn's hand, sliding my fingers through her own.

She sucks in a breath.

My grip involuntarily tightens at the sound.

"Trust me?" I ask.

She nods.

I pull her along behind me—past Graham and Piper; past Jeremy and Sarah; and past Kyle, who glares at me while grinding his marshmallow stick into the snow-covered ground—across the empty interstate and into the trees. If I were a better man, I might care that this is killing him, but if all is fair in love and war, then I won't let Evelyn choose him without putting up a fight.

A few people follow us, but I know these fields better than anyone. We zig and zag through rows of pines, into the deepest parts, where branches interlock and stretch out onto the pathways, making them nearly too thin to move through. These are the wild trees, the ones that have been allowed to grow tall for the few wealthier families who visit the farm every year, to reach the tops of the twenty-foot ceilings in their great rooms and libraries.

Evelyn laughs behind me, and I put my fingers to my lips, making a shushing sound, even though I'm laughing right along with her.

In the distance, we hear Jeremy call, "Ready or not, here I come!" But he's still far enough away, and the rest of the world is quiet around us, without even the sound of other people running by. We don't have to hide yet. We walk between the trees, our shoulders bumping every few steps.

Evelyn takes a deep breath. "I love this smell."

I grin. "You wouldn't love it so much if it seeped into

all of your clothes."

Her gaze slides to the unbuttoned coat I picked up at a Salvation Army back home and the ridiculous Christmas sweater underneath. "I don't know. I think it'd make them smell nice."

My heart beats faster. "Tell me something about yourself, Evelyn Waverley."

She laughs. "What do you want to know?"

"Anything." *Everything*. "Why do you love *Pride and Prejudice* so much?"

She looks down at the ground. "You don't want to know that."

"Yes," I say. "I do."

She blows out a breath, pushing her hands into her coat pockets. "My aunt Allison gave me her copy after some boy made fun of me for winning the fifth-grade science fair."

"Jerk."

"Yeah."

"I assume he's in our class?"

She nods.

"Want me to beat him up for you?"

She laughs. "I'll let you know."

Our boots snap the frost-covered grass.

"Let me guess. She gave you *Pride and Prejudice*, and you fell in love with Darcy."

"Yes," she says, smiling and staring up at the stars. "And no. I fell in love with the whole thing. All of the characters, the language, the setting—the fact that their problems seemed simpler somehow, or maybe they just handled them better than I could at that age." She shrugs. "They made me brave. Made me feel like I could be myself, even when people make fun of me for it."

I grit my teeth at the thought of anyone hurting her. "Does that happen a lot? People making fun of you?"

"Not a lot, no. At least, not in any outright way. But they'll make comments about how I need to lighten up. Not take things so seriously. Have fun. And I think they mean well—and sometimes they're right—but I also want them to realize that I'm right too. That there's nothing wrong with wanting to be productive. That maybe I was made this way for a reason."

"World changer." The words float out of my mouth the second I think them.

"What?"

"That's how I've always seen you, as someone who's going to change the world someday. You shouldn't feel sorry for having the ability to get three times as much done in a day as a normal human being. You should celebrate it, and other people should too. If it was making you miserable, sure, I could see why people would tell you to slow down, but it's like..." I pause, afraid I've revealed too much.

She turns to me. "Yes?"

I hesitate. Clear my throat again. "It's like you come alive when you're in the middle of a project. Like you're more alive than anyone I've ever met. The only time you seem miserable is at things like these, when you can't do what you want to do."

"Doesn't that make me kind of terrible though? That I want to be able to do things *my* way, on my own timetable?"

"You shouldn't apologize for how you're wired, Evelyn, and you do make an effort. It's not like you blow everyone off."

She opens her mouth, and I can see the argument already forming in her eyes.

"Look at that night at the ice cream shop," I say. "We were there to work, but you pushed that aside to make that gingerbread house with me. And look at tonight." I bump her shoulder on purpose this time. "Twister champ."

Maybe it's just the cold air biting her cheeks, but I

swear she blushes when I mention it.

"That's only because—" She cuts her gaze to me.

"Because?"

She shakes her head. "Forget it."

"Aw, come on. You have to know that telling me to forget it means I'm going to badger you until you tell me."

"Leave me alone," she says, laughing and power walking ahead of me.

"Oh no you don't." I lunge forward and grab the puffy arm of her winter coat. She laughs harder as I pull her back and she stumbles into me. Her chest pounds into mine, and then she's staring up at me, and suddenly neither one of us is laughing.

Footsteps crunch the frost-covered grass a few rows away from us.

Evelyn's eyes widen.

I put my finger to my lips and smile. Then I take her hand and lead her to the base of a sixteen-foot spruce. I hold up a curtain of branches as we slide underneath them, tucking ourselves against the base of the tree. The branches envelop us, and there is just enough space between the cracking, frosted ground and the first layer of branches that we can lie down on our bellies with our elbows and heads propped up, our legs stretching out behind us. It takes a moment for my eyes to adjust to the darkness, but when they do, I see that Evelyn is smiling at me.

"I don't think anyone could find us in here," she whispers, her breath puffing little white circles into the air as she blinks up at the blue branches above us and the moonlight just barely filtering through.

"I hid under one of these once," I tell her, the words forming before I can decide if it's something I even want to share. "When I was nine. It was the only time my mom and I visited. She needed money to make rent, and I guess she thought Uncle Bill and Aunt Bee would be more likely to give it to her if she made an effort to visit."

Evelyn is quiet for a moment.

Then: "Why did you hide?"

The way she asks it, hesitant, unsure if she should pry, lets me know that she understands—from my tone or the words themselves—that the answer is one I may not want to give.

My throat feels like it's been scraped raw with sandpaper, and my heart flaps like wings against my ribcage. My mind races, listing all the reasons I shouldn't tell her—because she'll look at me differently; because if you don't show someone the real you, it can't hurt as bad when they reject you, because they're only rejecting an idea of you. But for some reason, when I'm around her, I feel my defenses slipping. I *want* to tell her.

"Mom was using again. She was trying to hide it from Uncle Bill and Aunt Bee, but a needle fell out of her pocket while she was helping out at the tree lot, and the second I saw it hit the ground, it was like the whole world froze. Bill and Bee stared at it, along with all of the customers who were there that day, and then they glared at her, and I just knew that whatever was about to happen, I didn't want to be there to see it. So, I took off." I swallow. "You know, no one even realized I was gone until almost an hour later. Bill was the one who found me. I'd fallen asleep under the branches. It was a smaller tree than this one, a little closer to the gift shop. My feet must have been poking out."

"What did he say?"

"Nothing. He just scooped me up and carried me home. My mom and I left the next day. She didn't tell me if they gave her the money or not, but we managed to stay in that apartment for six more months after that, so I'm assuming they did."

"Is that why you came here? Because of your mom?"

I pull my fingers, stiff and purple with cold, back into the cuffs of my coat. This truth is one that is not as easy to give away. "Something like that."

She shifts, and I don't know if it's on purpose, but she's an inch closer to me, her leg nearly pressing against mine. The sensation, the physical energy that pulses between us, makes my entire body ache.

*Steady.*

Feet pound across the grass beyond our pine-needle veil. At first, I think it's Jeremy, but then I hear Graham's voice, teasing Piper because she brought a book with her to hide with.

"I didn't bring it with me to hide with," Piper whispers back. "It was already in my coat."

"Well, you won't have time to read it if I have anything to say about it," Graham replies, grabbing at the hem of her coat and spinning her toward him.

"Graham!" she squeals, playfully pushing him away.

"Come, my lady," he says, scooping her up. "I shall carry you to literary safety, where you may read your book in peace whilst we await our inevitable capture."

She squeals again, louder this time, as Graham races through the trees, carrying her in his arms.

Evelyn shifts again. A millimeter closer. It takes everything I have inside of me not to close the distance between us.

"Now that I've shared that embarrassing part of myself," I say, trying to lighten the mood, "I think it's only fair you tell me what you were going to say earlier."

"When?" she asks.

"When you were going to reveal why you decided to school me in Twister."

"No thanks."

"Don't make me kick you off my tree."

She rolls onto her side to look at me more fully. "Oh, so it's your tree now?"

My body moves in relation to hers, mimicking her. "My family does own it."

"Touché."

"Well?"

"Well." She takes a deep breath. "To be honest, I did those things because of you."

"Because you felt sorry for me?"

She runs her index finger through the pine needles, absently drawing a figure eight. "Because when I'm with you, my mind goes sort of...quiet. Like I can actually turn it off. Or—not turn it off, I guess. It's more like my thoughts get"— she meets my gaze—"redirected."

A beat passes.

"Evelyn?"

She inhales. "Yes?"

"Can I kiss you?"

And it feels like days, weeks, *months* pass as I wait for her answer, but then, there in the darkness, beneath an evergreen curtain and the moon and the stars beyond, comes the sweetest, softest, most amazing sound I've ever heard:

"Yes."

## 22

## Evelyn

### ✳✳✳

*B*eckett moves closer to me, his arm wrapping gently around my waist, pulling me toward him. His breath comes out in shudders, like he's just as terrified and uncertain as I am, not because it feels wrong, but because it feels so, *so* right.

He presses his forehead against mine, giving me one more second to say no, to pull away, but I've never wanted anything more in my life than I want Beckett Hawthorne to kiss me, here, now, on a blanket of brown pine needles, completely hidden in a world of our own making.

He closes his eyes.

His nose brushes mine.

And then his lips, soft as down feathers and smooth as satin, press against my own. He tastes like golden marshmallows and melted chocolate, and that scent that is uniquely his—pine needles and winter air and sandalwood cologne—mixes with the campfire smoke clinging to both of our clothes as he leans his body against mine.

Warm. He's so warm.

He deepens the kiss, and what started as soft, hesitant, questioning, turns wild. Clawing. Feral. I push my fingers into his hair. He presses his mouth hard against mine.

I didn't know kissing could be like this. Like devouring the other person. Like disappearing inside of each other and becoming one mind, one soul, one body.

His hands trace the small of my back. I wrap my arms inside his open coat, my own fingers memorizing the pattern of his spine. He breaks the kiss, moving his lips to my neck. My name is part groan, part growl on his tongue—"*Evelyn,*"—and nothing has ever sounded so amazing as the desperation raking his voice, like he's still terrified. Of himself. Of me. Of whatever is happening between us.

I'm scared too. I've never wanted anything this badly, and it feels so delicate, like it could all go up in wisps of smoke and tattered dreams. Like it's a magical thing, one not of this world, and I have to find some way to bottle it tight before it disappears.

The sound of running feet startles us. We've rolled toward the edge of our refuge, so our feet are sticking out of the curtain. We have just enough time to break apart before Jeremy pokes our legs with a stick.

"Gotcha!" he says.

Beckett and I stare at each other, our breathing rough, questions swirling in both of our eyes.

If anyone notices how ruffled we look as we head back to the bonfire, or how we sound like we just finished the hundred-yard dash, or how we can't look at each other, but we also can't leave each other's side, they don't say anything.

It takes me off guard, how the world around me still looks the same, but inside, *my* world has shifted.

I'm in love with Beckett Hawthorne.

But he's a gust of wind roaring down a highway. A wandering soul. A *damaged* soul. One that can't be tied down. And I know in that instant, as we melt back into the group and he puts space between us again, rebuilding the wall we just tore down, that he is going to break my heart.

And for as strong as I've always felt—as strong as I've always made myself out to be—I don't think anyone could survive having their heart broken by Beckett Hawthorne.

At some point, he is going to leave.

And he's going to take every last piece of me with him.

### ✳✳✳

The party slows down around ten, when most of the cast have to head home for curfew. My parents have never actually set a curfew for me, mostly because I only leave the house for the rare sleepover at Isla's or Savannah's. They know I love my routine too much to mess with it by being out late. We're early-to-bed, early-to-rise sort of people, so there's a good chance Mom and Dad are already asleep, trusting me to get home any minute now, which means I could technically stay out until three o'clock in the morning and neither of them would know the difference.

I don't know if Beckett has a curfew, but he's the type of boy who would know how to get around one even if he did.

I help Aunt Bee clear crumbs off end tables and collect holiday mugs strewn throughout the first floor as the rest of the cast leaves, stopping to give me hugs and promising they'll have their lines memorized by the end of next week.

Kyle is the only one who doesn't say goodbye, and even though I know whatever is going on with Beckett can't lead anywhere good, I also know my soul will never tie itself to Kyle the way it has to Beckett, and letting Kyle hope otherwise is the cruelest, most selfish thing I could ever do, even if

the logical part of my brain says I'd be better off with someone like Kyle than I ever could be with someone like Beckett.
But whether Beckett stays or leaves, Kyle will never be to me
what Beckett has so quickly and irrevocably become.

The second we manage to find a moment alone together
I have to tell Kyle the truth.

I find Beckett at the sink, his shirtsleeves pushed up to his
elbows as he dips coffee mugs into a warm, soapy bath on
one side and washes them off in the other. I bring the last of
the mugs over, then hold out a towel and offer to dry. Beckett
smiles and hands the washed mugs to me, our fingertips
brushing with every exchange.

Aunt Bee strolls back into the kitchen tying a dark-green
scarf around her neck that perfectly accents her red coat.
She really is a walking Christmas ad, and she has the knowing twinkle in her eye to match.

"Well, kids, I'm off," she says, crossing the kitchen to peck
Beckett's cheek. "Thanks for being a good sport."

Beckett shrugs as he reaches for the pot that held the
cider and dunks it into the sink.

I love how Aunt Bee smiles at him, full of all the love and
light of a parent. His Uncle Bill looks at him the same way.
It's softer, less overt, but it's there. It makes me wonder if
Beckett even realizes how much he is loved in this house.

Aunt Bee sidles up to me next, giving me the kind of
hug that makes you feel like you're being wrapped up in a
giant, fuzzy blanket.

"You two be good," she says.

My cheeks warm.

Beckett and I both tell her good night. Then we turn back
to the sink, working quietly until her headlights, spotlight-
ing the backyard through the kitchen window, disappear,
and the sound of her tires falls away.

Beckett's uncle went to bed hours ago. It's just the two

of us.

Beckett hands me one pot to dry, then another.

Neither one of us knows what to say.

The instrumental Christmas music Aunt Bee put on earlier is still playing, a piano version of "I'll Be Home for Christmas" thrumming softly through the darkened space, and the only light emanates from the single bulb over the kitchen sink and the multicolored, dappled glow from the dining room Christmas trees slicing across the floor. The wind whistles against the windowpane as a few flurries begin to fall.

"Looks like the freakishly cold December is going to continue," I say, angling my head toward the window, and I hate how strained my voice sounds, how obvious it is that I'm grasping for anything to talk about.

He doesn't answer, and my heart pounds in my chest. Does he regret the kiss? Is he trying to think of a way to let me down easy? Is my heart going to get broken before it's even had a chance to enjoy the ride?

But then he moves to stand behind me, his arms wrapping around my arms, helping me dry the last pot. The feeling of him there, pressed against me, sends electric shocks all the way down to my toes. He tilts his head and inhales the scent of my shampoo.

"I love the way you smell," he murmurs before kissing my neck again, his stubble tickling my jaw in the most amazing way.

I spin around to face him, the sharp edge of the counter pressing into the small of my back. Beckett keeps his knuckles against the countertop, pinning me between his arms, and I flash back to him doing the same thing during Twister and wonder if it makes me weak, the fact that I love being enveloped by him.

"What are we doing?" I ask.

His hair falls into his eyes in that way that I love. "I don't know."

I'm staring at his lips again. Remembering how soft they are. How they make my entire body melt into his.

He grips the edge of the counter. The muscles in his forearms tighten, and my gaze traces the curving lines of them. He bites his lower lip, like he's fighting the urge to do something very inappropriate.

"You should go," he says, his voice rough.

"What if I don't want to go?"

He closes his eyes. "Evelyn."

I push his hair back. "Beckett."

He threads his fingers through mine, then angles his head toward the stairs. I nod.

Somewhere above us, Uncle Bill coughs.

My eyes widen.

"Don't worry," Beckett tells me. "I caught him sneaking brandy into his cocoa. A megaphone to the ear wouldn't wake him."

I follow him up the narrow, creaky steps, set at a sharp incline so it's more like climbing a ladder than ascending a flight of stairs. I hold on tight to his hand so I won't fall.

"How does Bill climb this thing every day?"

"Muscle memory," Beckett answers.

The second floor is dark, with only shards of blue moonlight filtering through the windows and doorframes. Beckett tugs my hand to the right, and we step into his room. He flips on the light, revealing what looks like a guest room overtaken by a teen boy, with a shirt tossed on top of the royal blue, diamond-patterned comforter draped across the unmade bed; a makeshift desk crafted out of a low dresser and a folding chair, with a computer that looks like it came from the Dark Ages; a stack of creased paperbacks teetering on the bedside table beneath an antique floral lamp (a quick

glance reveals author names I'm not surprised to see: Ray
Bradbury, J.D. Salinger, Hunter S. Thompson, and ones that
I am: Ralph Waldo Emerson, Wendell Berry, T.S. Eliot); and
a pile of dirty laundry on the floor.

Beckett pulls the shirt off the bed and kicks the pile of
laundry into the closet, right next to a black violin case.

"Will you tell me why you don't play anymore?" I ask him,
angling my head toward the closet.

His Adam's apple rolls down his throat as he stares at it.
For a second, I don't think he's going to answer me, but then:
"It was the time in my life that I was the happiest. My mom
got us an apartment in a not-great part of San Antonio and
worked at a high-end grocery store by the River Walk. She
was clean—or as clean as she gets. Clean enough to keep
our lives together anyway."

He sinks down on the edge of the mattress, rubbing his
hands over his face. An exhausted groan escapes his lips.
Then he moves his hands down, clasping them in front of
him, staring at a spot on the floor. The next words seem hard
to get out. I take a seat next to him and—hesitantly—put my
hand on his back.

He relaxes under my touch.

"We couldn't have afforded lessons anywhere if it weren't
for the staff at my elementary school, let alone lessons at the
San Antonio Music Conservatory, but my second-grade music teacher said I had a gift, and she collected money from
the whole school so I could go. My teacher, Mr. Forsyth, paid
for my violin. I was the youngest student there—and the
only one who couldn't afford to pay for anything. But none
of that mattered to Mr. Forsyth or to anyone else. They said
I was a prodigy." He says this last word as if he's never heard
anything more ridiculous.

"Were you?" I whisper.

There's something about this conversation that suddenly

feels sacred despite his self-deprecating tone.

"I could play classical music while most kids my age were just learning how to pull the bow across the strings, so I guess in that way, I did okay. They even asked me to perform in their annual Christmas concert when I was ten. Tchaikovsky's Violin Concerto. Second movement."

"How did it go?"

He shrugs. "There was a standing ovation."

I smack his back. "Beckett. Seriously? And you want to sell it to buy a car?" I lean forward, trying to meet his gaze, but he keeps staring at the floor. "Why don't you play anymore? I know you said moving so much made it difficult, but I'm sure you could've figured out a way."

A muscle in his jaw ticks. "Mom got back into hard drugs not long after we moved to Boulder. I tried to keep playing, but we couldn't afford lessons anywhere. Mr. Forsyth liked to call and check up on me, but when we moved again, I didn't give him our new number. I knew it was pointless."

"There's nothing pointless about developing your God-given gifts."

"You've never heard me play. I could be horrible for all you know."

"Um, standing ovation? At a legit conservatory? In a huge city, at a concert where tickets probably cost a couple hundred bucks a pop? You're right, that's a big assumption on my part."

Beckett doesn't laugh.

I arch a brow and push backward on the bed, crossing my legs underneath me. "Fine. Then play for me."

"What?"

"Play for me. That's the only way I'll know if you're any good."

"I don't think so."

"Why not?"

"I haven't picked up a violin in years."

"I'm not looking for perfection. I just want to know if I'm right."

He narrows his eyes at me. "I'll wake Uncle Bill."

"You said yourself a megaphone to the ear wouldn't wake him. Now go ahead and play. You've run out of excuses."

I hold my breath, waiting for his reply.

He mumbles something, but then he gets up, crosses to the closet, and brings the case back, setting it on the edge of the bed. He reaches for the clasps.

Hesitates.

I sit up straighter.

He inhales, and then opens the case.

The most beautiful violin I've ever seen sits inside, all gleaming mahogany, with a curved handle at the top that looks like a piece of delicate scrollwork. Beckett takes it out and spends several minutes tuning the strings. I sit in the middle of his bed, unmoving. I'm afraid I'll spook him if I even so much as breathe too loudly.

And then he lifts the violin, places his chin on the rest, tilts the bow against the strings, and, with a deep breath, begins to play.

The melody is haunting—long, drawn out notes that speak of grief and heartache and soul-wrenching loss. His fingertips curve over the neck of the violin, moving up and down the strings with precision, as if the composition were written on the backs of his eyelids. His brow scrunches and he is transported to another place entirely, and I can see him, the kid who received a standing ovation, who found what he was created for just to have it all snatched away by circumstances completely out of his control.

I always suspected there was a reason for the darkness in Beckett, for the ways his shoulders draw down and his neck dips when he feels uncomfortable, like if he could only take up less space, be less intrusive, less alive, then maybe he could get through whatever is happening around him unscathed. But I never thought the darkness would be an addicted mother and an uprooted, poverty-stricken childhood. It's no wonder Beckett wants to run away. I imagine the farthest corners of the world would not be far enough for him.

Tears prick my eyes as the notes climb higher and then fall, as if jumping from a cliff, swooping and soaring and cascading and crashing. Beckett never once opens his eyes. It's as if he is willing the music to life from the deepest parts of himself.

It is both captivating and heartbreaking to watch.

He ends on a final note that pulls across the strings slowly, rhythmically humming into the pockets and corners of his room.

Beckett opens his eyes.

A breath escapes my lips, one I didn't know I'd been holding.

"You can't sell your violin." Tears break from my lashes. "I'll find some way to get you the money for a car if you really need one, but please. Don't throw this part of you away. It's too beautiful, too pure, too—"

I cut myself off, shaking my head because I can't find the words to describe the way the innermost parts of me felt pulled into the music, called into being, into *remembering*, into a primal place where the meaning of life is hidden, if only we could find some way to reach out and grab it.

"You have a gift, Beckett." I don't wipe the tears away. He needs to see—needs to know—how special he is. "You can't give it up."

"Who's going to stop me?" He arches a brow like he's joking, but he looks taken aback.

"I am." I push up off the bed to stand in front of him,

taking the hand that had been holding the strings into my own, running my fingers over his callouses. "So this is what these are from."

He swallows. "It's been six years since I last practiced on my own...since my mom told me we were never going back to the conservatory...and they're still there."

I don't know what makes me so brave. Maybe it's the music or the way he's looking at me like all he's ever wanted was to be seen, known, understood. Whatever it is, I bring each fingertip to my lips and kiss them, one by one. Then I cup his cheek in my hand and meet his gaze.

"Beckett, this is what you're meant to do."

He stares at me for a moment like he wants to believe me, but then he averts his gaze and moves away from me, stuffing the violin back in its case. "If that were true, I would've been born into a family that could afford it."

"Beckett—"

"Leave it, Evelyn."

"But—"

He slams the case closed. "I said *leave it*."

I take a step back, stricken.

His gaze softens. "I'm sorry, I just...I can't think about any kind of life where this might have been something I was meant to do because that's not my life. It's too painful to pretend otherwise."

"But there are scholarships," I murmur. "You're good enough to get every single one of them."

He doesn't answer.

"I'll drop it," I say, "if you promise to at least think about it."

He clears his throat. "Yeah. Okay."

My lips twitch into a quick smile. There and gone.

He reaches for me, wrapping his arm around my waist and pulling me against him.

"I'm sorry." He presses his forehead against mine one more

time, then murmurs, "Come on. I'll walk you to your car."

And even though everything inside of me is telling me this is a mistake, that I can't lose myself in a boy, especially one whose picture should be beside the word *heartbreaker* in every dictionary, I fall in love with the feeling of his hand holding mine. With the way his knuckles and his veins and his bones stand out, leading to the edges of his tattoo on his wrist. With the way he always looks so serious, like one wrong move, one mistake, will break his entire world, and so he's measuring every step, every thought, every word, every gesture.

I can't believe there was ever a single second where I thought I couldn't stand Beckett Hawthorne.

Allison was right. He *is* my Mr. Darcy.

But nothing about this—about *him*—screams happily ever after.

In so many ways, this relationship feels broken before it even begins, and that's why, even as I feel my heart and soul and entire being inextricably tying itself to him, my hands shake and my knees feel weak, because suddenly I feel like I have everything to lose, and for a girl who loves controlling every outcome, that is a terrifying thing.

I have no control here.

And that scares me most of all.

# 23

## *Beckett*

### ✳✳✳

*S*unday morning dawns crisp and cold, with the frost that formed last night sparkling like thousands of tiny crystals in the early morning sunlight. A few flurries fall down around us as I follow Uncle Bill to his truck. He has some errands to run in town before the lot opens at ten, so he offered to drop me off at rehearsal. I gladly took him up on it. I know Evelyn would have picked me up if I'd asked her, but I've been so messed up since last night, I need a minute away from her to think, to get my bearings, to remember why falling in love with her is such a bad idea, because God knows I can't remember it when she's standing right in front of me, looking like the answer to every whispered prayer.

I'm so close to finishing up my hours, so close to my eighteenth birthday, so close to freedom, it has become a living, breathing thing, pulsing in the distance, growing ever closer. It's all I can think about—the knowledge that once I'm free, I can finally choose my own life. Who I hang out with,

what I do, where I go—no one else will be able to dictate
it for me. I've spent years dreaming of the day I can leave
everything behind, but now, with Evelyn, I don't know what
I want anymore. She muddles everything up. I can't think
clearly when I'm with her.

I know what it feels like to not have a single say in your
own life. Control is all I've ever wanted, so the fact that every
part of me feels completely *out* of control when I'm with
Evelyn terrifies me even more than the thought of juvie did.
And yet I can't stop myself from seeing her. It's like we're
magnets, drawn to each other so that every step I take away
from her, every centimeter of distance, resists me, like trying
to move through sludge.

She makes me forget how dangerous it is to give yourself
to someone, to lose yourself in them. And that terrifies me
most of all.

I'm one of the last cast members to arrive. I take my usual
seat in the second row, tugging off my jacket and the black
scarf Aunt Bee knitted for me and placed on my desk without saying a word. Evelyn is sitting on the edge of the stage,
completely in her element with her three pens in her hand
and the purple one behind her ear, talking something over
with Graham and Jeremy about staging in the third act. I
lean forward, crossing my arms on the chairback in front of
me and resting my chin on my wrists, watching her.

I want to tell her how much last night meant to me.
How much *she* means to me. I want to tell her that I'm
scared, that I've never had any real or lasting thing in my
life, that anyone I've ever cared about has disappointed me.
Well, except for Aunt Bee and Uncle Bill, but give someone
enough time and they'll inevitably do something to hurt
you; I've become convinced of that.

I want to tell her we should probably end this now before either of us gets hurt.

I want to ask her to never leave my side.

But none of this comes out of my mouth when she meets my gaze and jumps off the stage to sit in the seat in front of me, wearing a smile big and warm enough to melt a glacier.

For me.

She's smiling because she's happy to see me.

"Hey, you," she says, and my heart leaps toward her like a golden retriever.

"Hey," I reply.

"We're going to start with the last scene today, after Mr. Bennet has given his blessing for Darcy and Elizabeth to marry and everyone is gathered around the Christmas tree, singing carols. It's not really historically accurate, since the British didn't start putting up Christmas trees until a few decades later, but I think the audience will give us a little wiggle room there," she says, laughing under her breath in the most adorable way. "After that, the rest of the cast's voices will fade, and the spotlight will be on the two of us having this private conversation about, well"—she clears her throat—"when we first fell in love."

She blushes like she's said too much.

I reach for her hand, taking it in mine and turning it over to kiss the back of her hand.

She swallows. "Are you ready?"

My throat goes dry because I would follow Evelyn Waverley anywhere.

I nod and she calls everyone up onstage.

This scene does not happen during Christmas in the book—that's something Evelyn changed to fit the holiday season. Uncle Bill donated the live tree that Graham is now wheeling out onto the stage, strung with garland made from popcorn, cranberries, bay leaves, and dried orange slices. There are also fake candles with flickering electric lights swirling up the tree and presents wrapped in brown paper underneath. The Bennets and Mr. Bingley all circle the tree, singing "O Come, All Ye Faithful" while Evelyn and I stand off to the side, behind an old-fashioned couch that was donated by the local antique store. Just as Evelyn described, the cast's singing gets softer as the light around them dims and the spotlight focused on Evelyn and me brightens.

"There is one question I have for you, Mr. Darcy," Evelyn begins as we stand with our arms touching and our heads bent toward each other.

My voice is scratchy as I reply, "And what is that, pray tell?"

"How could you begin to fall in love with me?" she asks. "I can comprehend your going on charmingly when you had once made a beginning; but what could set you off in the first place?"

I stare down into her sea-glass eyes—so clear, so warm, so brilliant—and something shifts inside of me. All of those times I spoke my lines to Evelyn, telling myself it was Darcy speaking to Elizabeth and not me speaking to her, I realize were a lie.

It's always been me.

It's always been her.

And when I say the next lines, I know them to be true.

"I cannot fix on the hour," I say, "or the spot, or the look, or the words, which laid the foundation. It is too long ago. I was in the middle before I knew that I *had* begun."

The scene goes on, with Elizabeth and Darcy discussing the events that transpired between them, leading to this moment, with a blessing from Mr. Bennet and a wedding on the way—"Now be sincere," Evelyn asks, a coy smile tugging at her lips, "did you admire me for my impertinence?" and I respond from the very depths of my soul, "For the liveliness of your mind, I did,"—and I can no longer deny that everything has changed.

I no longer want to run away. No longer want to make a
life in some town I've never heard of, where no one will ever
bother me, and I can disappear into nothingness.

I want to be wherever Evelyn is. I want to go after those
scholarships. I want to be happy again.

And when our lines end and the spotlight dims and it is
just the glow of the candles on the tree and the last fading
notes of the Christmas carol being sung by the cast, I reach
up to gently cradle her face in my hands and press my lips
to hers. It's not in the script, but she tilts her head and kisses
me back, and then the rest of the cast and backstage crew
are clapping and whistling at us, not a single one of them
aware of the fact that my entire world has changed in the
span of a single second.

I no longer feel adrift.

I'm finally, blessedly, home.

# 24

## Evelyn

### ***

eckett waits for me as everyone packs up and leaves. It was our best rehearsal yet, and I'm beaming from the high of it. So many people knew their lines, and I could tell others were only a few more days away from not needing their scripts anymore. We ran through the entire third act twice without any issues, and with just one more week before we begin dress rehearsals, I feel like we're finally in a good place.

I stuff my script and notes into my backpack. Beckett comes up behind me, pulling the purple pen out from behind my ear and handing it to me.

"I always forget that one," I say, our fingertips brushing as I take it from him.

"I know," he replies. "It's adorable."

Something has changed in him. There's a lightness to him now, as if he's sloughed away the hardened layers of himself, built up over years of disappointments and heart-

break. It's not all gone—there's still armor there, still walls
that need to tumble—but he looks freer than I've ever seen
him, and the way he reaches for me, pulling me against
him and locking his arms around my stomach, hugging me
close, feels like a miracle. I melt into him, the one place I
feel safe to just be me.

"Come to the farmhouse tonight," he whispers in my
ear, sending tingling goosebumps down my neck. "Bee's
bringing a pot roast over for dinner, and we can watch a
movie after. Your pick."

I glance back at him, arching my brow. "*Pride and Prejudice*?"

"You mean you're not sick of it at this point?"

I shake my head. "Never."

He laughs, a real, full-bodied laugh, and it is the most
beautiful sound I've ever heard. "Which version?"

"The Keira Knightley one," I tell him. "It's not the more
popular one within the fandom—that honor belongs to the
Colin Firth adaptation—but I love the landscape shots. It
makes me want to live in a village in England surrounded
by misty fields, where I can take long walks every day and
think deep thoughts."

"Sounds perfect," he says, turning me in his arms to face
him. "Can I join you there?"

My breath catches. "I thought you had big plans to buy a
car and Kerouac your way across the country?"

His gaze deepens, his brown eyes warm as melted
chocolate. "I actually thought I'd follow your advice.
Apply for some scholarships." He clears his throat. "Go
wherever you go."

"To college?"

He nods.

I smile. "I'd like that."

"So, tonight? Around six?"

"I'm there," I tell him.

He exhales, relieved, like he wasn't completely sure I'd say yes, but how could I ever say no to him, this mysterious boy who's turned my life upside down in the most amazing and unexpected of ways?

"Do you need a ride?" I ask as I slip into my coat.

"If you don't mind."

I grab my backpack, but Mrs. Warren's voice echoes from her backstage office, stopping me. "Evelyn, could you come here for a moment?"

Beckett kisses my brow. "I'll wait for you in the atrium."

I squeeze his hand, then call back to her, "Coming!"

I ascend the stairs two at a time, feeling so light, I swear I could fly. There's a ridiculous grin on my face, and I'm practically bouncing with every step. Mrs. Warren looks up from her desk as I approach.

"You have every right to be happy," she says. "Everything is coming together beautifully."

"Huh?" It takes me a second to realize she means the play. "Oh, yes. I think we've got a really good shot at it being the best Christmas production our school has ever put on."

"I completely agree."

I lean against the doorframe. "So, what's up?"

She pulls out a sheet of paper with a graph on it. It looks like a log of some kind, with her handwriting looping across the columns in blue ink. There's a row for comments and a row for hours, with most of them saying *3:00 p.m.–6:00 p.m.* or *8:00 a.m.–12:00 p.m.*—the same as our rehearsal times.

"I'm just marking down Beckett's community service hours," she says, "and his social worker asked if I could include the hours he spent at the toy drive yesterday in my log, but I need your signature next to it since you were the one who was with him."

I take the paper from her, completely confused. The

words *community service hours* and *social worker* dart
through my head like tadpoles, impossible to catch. Under
the comments section is a recurring line in Mrs. Warren's
handwriting that says, *Play Rehearsal, Play Rehearsal, Play
Rehearsal,* and then, for yesterday, *Children's Hospital Toy
Drive,* along with the hours Beckett spent there helping me.

"What is this?" I ask.

Mrs. Warren's brow furrows. "It's the log for his community service hours, dear. You know, the ones he's been getting
for being in the play?" She leans back in her seat. "I must
say, I was surprised when his social worker told me that
the play could count toward them, but it's nice that this ar-
rangement has been so mutually beneficial for everyone,
don't you think?"

I glance up at her, and she must see the confusion in
my eyes.

"You did know about this, didn't you?" she asks. "You
and Beckett have been working so closely together, I just
assumed—"

"Yes," I say, quickly. "Yes, I knew. I just hadn't seen the
actual log. It's a lot of hours."

Mrs. Warren nods. "Aunt Bee says he'll be almost done
with them by the time the play is over. He might even hit
his number if we extend rehearsals leading up to the show,
like we've been discussing."

Aunt Bee knew about this. Mrs. Warren knew about
this. Beckett obviously knew about this. And yet not one
of them thought to include me.

All of this time, I thought he was doing the play for me,
to help me out, to make me happy. Just like I thought he
volunteered at the toy drive because he—I don't know—
wanted to spend time with me, or actually had the ability
to care about something other than himself.

But it was all a lie.

Everything he's done, he's done for himself. To get community service hours for some crime I wasn't even aware he committed. This whole time, I thought I was getting to know the real Beckett. That he'd been pulling his walls down. But I don't know the first thing about him.

I sign the paper, my fingers gripping the pen so tightly, my signature looks like a kindergartener's, all harsh, abrupt lines where there are usually soft, elongated loops. I hand the pen back without looking at her so she won't see the tears brimming in my eyes.

"Anything else?" I ask.

"No." Mrs. Warren sounds concerned, but she doesn't pry. "That's all. I'll see you tomorrow."

"See you tomorrow," I echo back, my voice breaking on the last syllable, but I turn on my heel and leave before she can say anything else.

I move across the stage and down the steps in a haze. *Muscle memory*, I remember Beckett saying last night as he glanced back at me with that smile that makes my heart quake, and suddenly my brain flashes through all of the times we've spent together, movie scenes playing across my mind.

He could have told me. There were *so many* times he could have told me.

Why didn't he? Did he think I wouldn't let him be in the play if I knew why he was doing it? Would I have trusted him less? I don't know the answer to that, but I do know that I can't trust a single thing he says now. He tells me he wants to get a scholarship and go wherever I go, but I could just as easily wake up tomorrow and find out he skipped town, and I would be shattered into a million tiny pieces so jagged they could never be put back together again, but I would not be the least bit surprised.

Beckett sees it on my face as I walk into the atrium. The

anger. The pain. The betrayal.

"What's wrong?" he asks.

My voice is thick. "Why didn't you tell me about the hours?"

He takes a step back, shaking his head like I've slapped him. "What?"

I'm crying in front of him for the second time in less than twenty-four hours, but this time, I *do* push the tears away, letting the anger flood me instead, because I hate that he did this to me, and the last thing I want him to know is just how badly he's hurt me.

"Why didn't you tell me that the whole reason you've been doing this play—the whole reason you offered to 'help out' at the toy drive yesterday—isn't because you *wanted* to, but because you were forced to? For *community service?*"

"Evelyn—"

"Because you've done us a real service, being the world's biggest jerk half the time—"

"And I apologized for that."

"Did you think it was funny?" In some, distant part of my brain I know I sound irrational, but it's quiet and small and has no power over the torrent of words building up in my throat. "Just an easy way for you to get your hours and leave? And if that was your plan all along, what was last night? A little bit of fun on the way out?"

"What? No, Evelyn, please—"

He starts toward me, but I push him away.

"Don't come anywhere near me. I actually *believed* you. You made me feel—"

*Special.*

*Beautiful.*

*Seen.*

"What?" he asks. "What did I make you feel?"

I swallow. "It doesn't matter. It was all a lie."

"None of it was a lie."

"It wasn't the truth."

"My feelings for you have always been true, Evelyn. And you're right, I lied about why I was doing it, but I don't really see why that matters."

"Because I don't know you, Beckett!" My voice reverberates through the empty atrium. "Because I don't know if anything you say is real."

He grits his teeth, and I watch every trace of the Beckett I knew melt away. I can practically see every single wall being rebuilt in his eyes, closing him off from me as a barely controlled rage rolls across his face, dark and foreboding as thunderclouds.

"You're one to talk," he grinds out, his tone suddenly harsh. "I've just been another project to you this whole time. Admit it."

"What? No, that's not—"

"Something to examine. A problem to figure out. I've got a little secret for you, Waverley," he says, his voice so cold, I shiver. "The know-it-all act gets old quick."

"Stop." The tears are falling fast now. "Just stop."

"You think you know me so well, that you've got me all figured out, but you haven't even asked me why I have to do community service in the first place."

I glare at him. "I assume it's for doing something selfish and immature."

He shakes his head, swearing under his breath. "I don't need this."

He starts for the door.

Stops.

Turns back.

And in a voice so low I have to strain to hear him, he says, "I was helping my mom."

"What?"

He meets my gaze, and I'm surprised at the tears rimming his own lashes.

"She got caught holding," he says. "Heroin. She was on parole, and I knew she was going to get locked up for a long time if they took her in. So I told the cops it was mine." He looks away. "The judge went easy on me. It helped that it was my first offense, and my social worker is an old friend of his. I think she managed to convince him that I was somehow worth another chance. What a joke." He laughs under his breath.

I take a step forward. "Beckett—"

"Whatever it was, he gave me community service instead of juvie, and Serena convinced him to let me serve my hours here in Christmas. She said it would be a better environment for me than the one I was in, and he agreed. But what neither of them counted on—what I didn't even know to expect—was you." He swallows. "This may have started out as a way to help myself, but it didn't end that way. You can choose to believe it or not, but it's the truth. You've helped me find myself again, Evelyn. You've made me want to be a better person." His eyes narrow as his voice hardens. "But all you see when you look at me is a selfish asshole who can't be trusted."

I bite my lip. "Beckett, *please*—"

"Don't try to deny it. It's written all over your face."

I don't say anything. Because for the first time since this whole messed-up conversation began, words fail me. My mind is a complete blank.

"Do me a favor," he says, moving toward the door.

"What's that?" The words feel like clay in my mouth. I have to force them out.

"Don't come over tonight."

He bumps open the door with his arm and pops the collar of his jacket up against his ears as he walks out into the snow, and even though I am standing, inside I'm collapsing, because I don't know how so much has changed between us in just the span of a few minutes.

I push the tears away. Tell myself it's better that this ended now, before we really got serious about each other, when the pieces of me lying broken on the floor aren't too shattered to knit back together.

But if I'm being honest, I'm not sure there's a single chance of knitting *anything* back together once Beckett Hawthorne has torn it apart.

✳ ✳ ✳

# 25

## *Beckett*

### ✳✳✳

I walk the whole way home, along the side of the interstate, the cold air seeping into my lungs.

I can't believe I thought she'd understand, that she wouldn't see me differently. But the second I saw her step into the atrium, I knew everything had changed. And the worst part about it was that she didn't even ask me to explain, just accused me of things that were horrible and unfair.

And also kind of true.

I *was* only thinking about myself when I joined the play. I had no reason—no *desire*—to join, other than maybe out of jealousy, seeing as I couldn't stand the way Kyle kept looking at her like she was his whole world, when I was so sure, even if I hadn't admitted it to myself yet, that she was only ever supposed to be mine. But still, was it so wrong that I'd wanted to complete my hours as quickly as possible, and that the play was the fastest way to do it?

*No, what was wrong was you didn't tell her the truth from*

*the beginning,* a small voice that sounds, not surprisingly, like Aunt Bee, echoes in the back of my mind.

*Because I knew she wouldn't look at me the same way,* I think back at her.

*She might have if you'd given her the chance.*

She proved to me tonight that I was right the first time.

*She proved to you that she has the ability to be hurt by you,* Aunt Bee's voice whispers back as I turn onto our road, the pine-green Christmas tree lot sign coming into view (*Welcome to Campbell Farms!* it says, with *Happy Holidays!* written underneath). *And people who feel hurt don't always say the kindest things.*

My own horrible words reverberate back to me.

*The know-it-all act gets old quick.*

I curse under my breath as I start up the gravel drive to the farmhouse.

Evelyn was right. I am an asshole.

Part of me feels like I should call her and apologize—for what I said, for what I did, for *everything.* But the other part is telling me that she knows the truth now and it's up to her to decide if she'll believe it or not.

Maybe it's better if she doesn't.

I don't know what I was thinking before. About the scholarships. About Evelyn. About a future that didn't involve me running away and starting a new life somewhere no one from the old one could ever find me. It was nothing but wishful thinking, and if I've learned anything in the almost-eighteen years of my life, it's that wishful thinking only turns into broken dreams and ghosts of what could have been.

They aren't worth a second of anyone's time.

I wrench open the door to the farmhouse's mudroom and slam it shut behind me. I'm already dressed for work, but I'm in no position to spread holiday cheer. I need to get out there—need the hours—but I'm going to try to get my head right first, starting with some push-ups to get the adrenaline out and some coffee to sharpen my focus.

But when I step inside, I see that I'm not alone.

Bill and Bee are sitting at the kitchen table, and there's a man occupying the chair that held my ugly Christmas sweater the night before—how was that only just last night when it feels like a million years ago?—wearing a familiar camel-colored motocross jacket and a sweat-stained baseball cap. He turns at the sound of my footsteps.

Roy.

"I told you I'd come for you, boy."

"Now you wait just a minute, Roy," Bill says, jamming his index finger into the table. "I already told you. Beckett's not going anywhere with you."

"He's my kid, Bill, and I'll take him wherever I damn well please."

"We'll just see what the sheriff has to say about that. He'll be here any minute."

"I've got parental rights."

"You're his stepfather, Roy, not his biological one, and I can smell the booze on you from here. All the sheriff will have to do is give you a breathalyzer test, and I have no doubt he'll lock you up for the night so you won't get back in that car and hurt someone."

Roy scoffs. "Even if he does, I can still collect my boy in the mornin'."

"It's not that simple, Roy, and you know it," Aunt Bee says, leaning forward and calmly folding her hands in front of her, while Uncle Bill sits next to her, looking like he could kill my stepfather at any second. "You have to go through Serena to relocate Beckett, and she has to go through the judge, and seeing as the last time Beckett showed up to court, he did so with a bruise on his jaw, I doubt the judge would allow him to return to you."

Roy narrows his eyes. "They never proved that was me."

"Only because I didn't give you up," I say through gritted teeth. I cross the room to stand directly in front of him, my entire body shaking. "You promised you'd leave me alone if I didn't tell them about that—or about all the other times you hit me."

"What's wrong with this country that a kid can't get disciplined by the rod no more? It's makin' boys soft is what it's doin'." He pins his red-laced eyes on me. "I should've hit you harder. Maybe it would've knocked some sense into you."

Bill stands so abruptly the table almost knocks over. "Get out of my house."

Roy doesn't move. "Not without my boy."

"I'm not your boy," I tell him, "and I'm not going anywhere with you."

Roy opens his mouth to respond, but a car door slams in the driveway.

"That'll be the sheriff," Bill says. "Now, Sheriff Gates and I go way back. I'm sure he'll let you go peacefully if you promise to leave and never come back. But if you force the issue, he *will* take you in for drunk driving, and I'm pretty sure one more of those and they'll revoke your license, won't they, Roy? And then you'll have to hitchhike your way home because there's not a chance in hell I'm buying you a plane ticket."

Roy narrows his eyes. "This isn't over."

"Oh no, Roy," Bill replies. "It very much is."

The sheriff knocks on the door as a formality, immediately opening it and walking right in.

"Everything all right here, Bill?" he asks.

Bill nods, once. "Roy was just leaving. Weren't you, Roy?"

Roy looks at me, his hands on his hips. The sheriff reaches for Roy's arm, but Roy pulls away from his grasp.

"I'm goin'." He starts for the door, then turns back to me. "You just remember who you are, boy. This house, these people—none of this fancy stuff is yours. They'll get rid of you the second they don't need you anymore." His breath reeks of cheap tequila and cigarettes as he leans forward. "You're gutter trash, and you'll always be gutter trash, and you'll die gutter trash, and there ain't a damn thing you can do about it."

I glare at him, letting every ounce of hatred I feel toward this man radiate off me. "Goodbye, Roy."

He looks me up and down, then shakes his head, unimpressed, and walks out the door. Sheriff Gates follows after him.

Aunt Bee comes around the table, taking my face in her hands. "It's not true, Beckett, you hear me? It's not true. Bill and I both love you dearly, and we will *always* be here for you. All of this is yours as long as you want it."

A lump forms in my throat. "Thank you."

"And you are not gutter trash. Look at me."

I do.

She brushes my hair out of my eyes. "You are a beloved soul created by God with a destiny and a purpose. You are loved and cared for, and your life will be what *you* make of it. Your past—the things people have done to you—it only has the power to define you if you let it."

I nod.

She hugs me tight. And then Bill does something I never thought he'd do.

He wraps his arms around both of us.

He doesn't say a word. Just holds on like he's scared I'll disappear.

And I hold him back, scared he will too.

## 26
### Evelyn

**✱✱✱**

*B*eckett doesn't show up for rehearsals the next day, and he doesn't answer his phone.

I lie and tell everyone he's sick and that we'll have to rehearse without him. Kyle beams at the thought of getting to say lines with me, and I can tell he's secretly hoping this is the moment he's been waiting for, when Beckett will prove to be the unreliable jerk everyone has made him out to be.

But is that really who he is? I'm so confused, I don't know what to think.

I try to focus on what I'm doing—on who has their lines memorized and who still needs to work on them; on whether the blocking feels natural or forced; on whether the sound effects Jeremy keeps dropping are as terrible as they seem—but my heart isn't in it. How can it be, when every beat echoes Beckett's name?

I called Aunt Allison last night in tears. I had already spoken to Isla and Savannah, but they weren't much help.

Like the proverbial angel on one shoulder and the devil on the other, Isla just went on about true love and happily-ever-afters, while Savannah countered with the science of hormones and the ability to choose who we love. Neither stance solved my problem because neither of them could speak to what I really needed to know:

Is Darcy really someone who can be loved, or did Jane Austen just make him seem that way? Are the readers who swoon over Darcy, as I've always done, the ones who understand that people are more than they appear? Or are we the foolish ones, the daydreamers, the romantics—and the critics who argue that he's a horrible jerk who doesn't deserve Elizabeth the ones who have been right along?

Aunt Allison was quiet as I explained everything to her, from all the ways I felt myself falling for Beckett Hawthorne to all the ways he lied. And then I heard her take a sip of her morning smoothie before she, very quietly, said, "People are like icebergs, Evelyn. The parts that we see at the top are the culmination of years of programming, creating all of that icy buildup underneath."

"What do you mean, 'programming'?"

"Parents, friends, teachers, circumstances, cultural expectations—they all play a part in building our brains, for better or for worse. It sounds to me like your Mr. Darcy has had a very terrible, uprooted adolescence, and all of that baggage is going to influence the decisions he makes and the way he reacts to things. If Jane Austen did Darcy any disservice, it's that she didn't give us more information about *why* he was the way that he was, but she did show us, quite beautifully, how Elizabeth changed him, and how he changed her. That's the whole point of it, right? That people are always growing, always learning, and that the right influences in our lives can make all the difference. So, the question you should be asking yourself isn't whether this one circumstance is proof Beckett can't be trusted, but whether he's someone you want to grow with."

I choked back tears. "But what if this is proof that he's only going to end up hurting me?"

"Loving anyone is a risk, Evelyn. But life without love is meaningless."

Those words echo in my mind as Kyle comes up to me at the end of rehearsals, slinging his backpack across his shoulder. "So, uh"—he clears his throat—"do you think Hawthorne will be better by opening night?"

I'm so distracted, replaying the conversation with Allison in my mind, that I shake my head, trying to clear it. "What?"

"You said he's sick, right? Do you think he'll be better by opening night?"

I can tell by the way he's asking that he knows Beckett isn't sick.

"Oh. Um." I swallow. "I hope so."

"Because if he isn't," he says, quickly, like he needs to get it out fast or he won't be able to say it at all, "I'm more than happy to take over. I've already got all of my lines memorized, and I've been taking notes on all of Darcy's blocking, and I've even been mouthing the lines along with Beckett from the audience, trying to figure out how I would maybe do it differently. Like, take the second to last scene, when Darcy proposes to Elizabeth. Well, I noticed you move toward Darcy and look up at him with this really, uh, wonderful look, and I thought it might be a good place for a, um"—he wipes his suddenly glistening brow—"a kiss."

I blink.

His smile wobbles. "What do you think?"

"Um, yeah. Maybe."

He exhales. "I just wanted you to know that I've been taking my role very seriously. I'm ready."

I nod because it *is* good to know, but try as he might, Kyle is not Darcy. He's Bingley, and out there somewhere is his Jane, but I am Elizabeth, and there's only one person for me.

Anything less would be unbearable.

And yes, true love is a risk, and it means trusting *all* of someone, not just the parts we can see above the surface, but everything else buried underneath, and doing that means there will be pain and heartbreak, but maybe, *maybe*, if we choose each other, if we grow together, like Allison said—

Maybe we'll actually have a chance at happily ever after.

"You know what, Kyle? That is all really, really great, and I would love to talk to you about it, but I have to go." I stuff my script and notebooks in my backpack, throw on my coat, and—

Stop.

Because Kyle needs an answer, and it isn't fair I've kept him waiting this long.

"Kyle," I say, meeting his gaze, "I really appreciate everything you've done for this play. I'm so thankful you've been such a dedicated understudy, and there is a really good chance you'll be the one playing Darcy come opening night, but as for your other question about me going out with you—"

He brightens. "Yeah?"

I take his hand in mine. "There is someone out there who is perfect for you, but that girl isn't me."

He swallows. "It's Hawthorne, isn't it?"

I nod.

His lips stretch into a smile that looks like a shrug. "I knew it the first time I saw you two together. I was just hoping I was wrong."

"I'm sorry."

He studies me, a flurry of emotions crossing his face, then bends down and kisses my cheek. "Go get him, Waverley."

I grin. "Thanks, Caldwell."

I wrap him in a hug. He pats my back, whispering, "Go," and then I'm flying across the stage, toward the back door leading directly out into the parking lot. My heart beats his name—BECK-ETT, BECK-ETT—and I can't ignore it any longer. I have to see him. I have to know whether he really cares for me the way I care for him. Whether he really did only want the hours or whether, maybe, somewhere along the way, he fell for me too.

*I actually thought I'd follow your advice. Apply to some scholarships. Go wherever you go.*

I burst through the door and make a run for my car, my boots crunching salt cubes with every step. I open my car door and slam it shut behind me. I start the engine and peel out of the nearly empty parking lot, my tires squealing beneath me.

I don't stop until I get to the Christmas tree lot. It's after six, and the sign in the gift shop window says *Closed*, but Beckett is still in there—I can see him through the frosted window, holding a clipboard and checking items off a list—so I park my car, say a quick, silent prayer (*Please God help me*), and head for the door, my heart slamming against my chest as if it's trying to run ahead of me, racing back to the boy who was always meant to have it.

# 27

## Beckett

## ***

Cold wind whistles across the windowpane as snowflakes create diamond-crusted patterns on the glass. It's inventory night, and the gift shop is warm and smells of cinnamon and pine needles. The repetitive task of checking items off of lists and marking down what needs to be restocked is almost enough to keep my mind from drifting back to Evelyn, but every glance at the window reminds me of us at the kitchen sink, the softness of her hair on my cheek, the warmth of her body pressed against mine, and it makes me falter every time, the realization that I'm only half a person when she's not with me.

How can that happen so fast? How can you so quickly become aware of the missing parts of yourself when the only person who can fill them walks into your life? And what do you do once they're gone?

How are you ever supposed to be okay again?

Bill took Bee into the city. They almost didn't go, nervous after Roy's unexpected visit, but the sheriff personally escorted Roy out of town, and Bill's had this dinner planned for weeks, although he only mentioned it to Aunt Bee a couple nights ago, saying there was something he wanted to discuss with her.

I accidentally found the ring last night. After Bee had left and Bill had gone to bed, I was double-checking the lock on the mudroom door and accidentally bumped his coat off the hook. The ring box fell out of the pocket. An antique circlet of sapphires surrounding a square-cut diamond sat inside of it, and I knew instantly there was no way I was letting them miss tonight.

Someone knocks on the door, breaking me out of my thoughts.

"Sorry," I yell over my shoulder. "We're closed."

Another knock.

Exhaling sharply, I set down the clipboard—I really need to convince Uncle Bill and Aunt Bee to switch to a tablet—and cross to the door. I glance out the window before opening it, a terrible vision of Roy standing on the doorstep flashing through my mind, but it's not Roy.

It's Evelyn.

I swallow and open the door.

"We're closed," I tell her.

"Yes, you said." She's shivering. "Can I come in anyway?"

I stand aside to let her pass.

She walks in, smelling of summer even as she trails in snow on her boots.

My chest tightens.

"We missed you at rehearsal today," she says, looking around at the merchandise, at the ornaments and the Christmas mugs and the decorative wreaths and pine boughs for sale.

Anywhere but at me.

I clear my throat. "I didn't think it was a good idea for me to show up. You know, after yesterday."

She's quiet for a moment. Taking it all in.

I lean against the door. Every single one of my protective walls are up, the very hairs on my arms bristling like spikes as a warning siren blares through my brain. It knows my heart can't take being rejected by Evelyn Waverley. I'll survive it, just as I've survived everything else, but it will be pure hell, and I don't know what I'll turn into once I'm on the other side of it.

"Did you really mean it?" she asks, hope shining bright as flares in her eyes.

My jaw clenches. "Mean what?"

She takes a breath. "When you said you wanted to pursue scholarships? To go to whatever college I go to?"

"I did."

She takes a step closer.

I stare at the floor.

"And when you said you took the fall for your mom— that was also true?"

She's even closer now. Only two steps away from our boots touching.

"Every word," I tell her, my heart squeezing painfully in my chest as I remember the way Mom didn't even fight it. How she let me ruin my life to save her own.

"Beckett."

It's the way Evelyn's voice cracks on my name that makes me look up.

Tears glisten in her eyes, twin pools reflecting the amber-gold lamplight. "I'm so sorry I didn't believe you. That I didn't even ask for your side of things. But I'm asking now. Has all of this—the play, the time you've spent with me— has it just been a way to get the hours you need?"

I want to reach for her, but I keep my hands locked

behind my back. "It started out that way, but it didn't end like that."

She takes another step.

Close enough to kiss.

"How did it end?" she asks.

I look away from her.

She lays her hand against my cheek, gently turning my face back to hers. I bristle out of habit, but then I'm leaning into the softness of her—the smell of her skin, the light scratch of her rounded nails—and that old feeling resurfaces, the one that wonders what it would be like to fall into her gravitational pull. To be protected. Cared for. Placed in perfect alignment.

Evelyn Waverley is the steady constant I've never had.

But is there anything I can offer her back? Or will I only drag her down?

I push away from the door. "It doesn't matter."

I'm halfway across the room when her voice stops me.

"Don't do this, Beckett. Don't push me away."

My entire body tightens.

"Fine," she says. "If you're not going to say it, then I will." She takes a deep breath. "I love you, Beckett."

All of the breath leaves my body as if someone sucker punched me in the stomach.

I turn toward her.

She takes a step forward. "I fell in love with you the day I met you. I tried to fight it after I overheard you telling Kyle you would never be interested in someone like me, and I told myself I hated you because it sounded so cruel, the way you said it, but really, I was heartbroken, because I was already drowning in you." She wrings her hands together and stares at a spot on the wall across from me, unable to meet my gaze. "And then you kept showing me this other side of you, and I didn't know which one was the real Beckett, so I kept trying

to fight it, because I was afraid of falling in love with someone who so clearly didn't want to be here, let alone someone
who said he'd never be interested in me. And maybe you
still don't want to be here—maybe I've messed everything
up and you're going to leave town the second you can, and
it's going to kill me, but it'll be worse if you leave before I
ever get the chance to tell you exactly how I feel."

I cross the distance between us. Reach out and hesitantly—*fearfully*—take her hands in mine.

"How do you feel about me?" I whisper into the quiet, so
certain this must be a dream, that she can't be saying these
things. I don't deserve them, and I know I should send her
away before I take her down with me, but there's this spot
of something that feels like hope burning in my chest, and
I can't stamp it out. It's flickering, growing, burning everything in its path. And I want to believe it's real.

Evelyn turns my hands over in hers, staring at the calluses on my fingertips.

"I am enamored with you," she whispers back. "I've never
been more aware of another human being in my entire life. I
feel every move you make, even when I'm not looking at you.
Every breath, every heartbeat—it's like I'm more attuned to
you than I am to myself. Like my body bends and shapes
itself to yours whenever we're in the same room together,
and when you're gone, it feels like you take me with you. I
didn't know love could feel like that—not until I met you."

I bend forward, placing my brow against hers. "It feels so
good to hear you say that."

She looks up at me, and I can't contain the energy pulsing within me any longer. I take her face in my hands
and kiss her until we're both breathless, until neither of
us knows up from down or left from right. She half sobs,
half moans as I deepen the kiss, and then we're stumbling
into the shelves. Merchandise crashes to the floor around

us, and all the while I'm telling her how much I love her. How I can't imagine a single second of my life without her in it. How I will go wherever she goes, just so long as I never have to spend another moment away from her. And I promise her I will be better, for her, for me, for *us*—no more secrets, no more lies. And I apologize profusely, over and over again, for calling her a know-it-all. I tell her I don't even know why I said it, because her efficiency and her intelligence and her quick-wittedness are some of the things I treasure most about her, along with her kindness and compassion and the fire that burns so brightly within her that it has also caught flame inside of me, and if she could only look inside of my brain for two seconds, she would see just how incredible she really is.

Evelyn's tears are salty on my lips, and she's laughing and breathing my name. I tell myself to stop, that if we keep going like this we'll go too far, too fast, and that is the last thing I want to do.

I'm going to move slow. I'm going to cherish her. I'm going to earn her love over and over again and pray that someday I may actually be worthy of it.

A car door suddenly slams in the parking lot, jolting us away from each other.

I laugh and lean my forehead against hers. Our breaths come fast and rough.

"Another customer?" she asks.

I nod. "They'll go away when they see the sign on the door."

But they don't go away. They knock, just like Evelyn did.

"We're closed," I yell, half thankful they made us stop before anything else could happen, and half hating them for it.

The knocking stops.

Evelyn and I smile at each other.

And then the window shatters.

# 28

## Evelyn

***

I see the baseball bat out of the corner of my eye a second before it hits the window. There is no time to scream, to warn Beckett of what's coming, but he envelops my body with his anyway as glass shards spray and slide across the floor.

"Told you I'd come back for you, boy."

Beckett snaps his head toward the voice, thick and slurring with booze. The man silhouetted in the broken window is wearing a beige leather jacket and a shredded blue baseball cap with the words *Fisher Scrap Yard* running across it in faded capital letters. His eyes are so bloodshot they look like cut cherries, and he wobbles as if he's standing on a storm-rocked ship, but the baseball bat is steady as he points it at Beckett.

"Come with me now," the man says, "and there won't be any trouble."

"Evelyn," Beckett murmurs as he turns completely toward the man, shielding me with his body. He takes slow steps back, pushing me with him, like he's trying not to spook a wild animal. "Stay behind me."

I can hear my heartbeat in my ears as adrenaline pumps through my veins, but the fear sharpens my focus, and a tip Sheriff Gates gave our sixth-grade class during D.A.R.E. week flashes through my mind. I slide my phone out of my pocket and dial 9-1-1. I hear the faint voice of the operator answer on the second ring, but I don't say a word. Hand shaking, I hold the phone out just enough behind Beckett in hopes that the officer can hear everything they're saying.

The look the man gives Beckett is feral; a predator closing in on its prey. "I'm givin' you one last chance, boy. Open this door and face me like a man. You won't like the consequences if you don't."

"I'm not going with you, Roy," Beckett tells him. He sounds so strong as he says it, so unafraid, even though every line of his body is strung like a jungle cat, prepared to protect what is his. "You remember what Bill said? About the sheriff?"

The man shakes his head, chuckling. "That sorry excuse for a policeman won't even realize I was here until you and I are in the next state over."

"The judge won't like that, Roy."

"He will if you tell him it was your idea."

"I'm not going to do that."

The man—Roy—nods as if finally seeing things clearly, even though he's stumbling back and forth so much now that I have to imagine he's seeing at least two Becketts standing in front of him.

"All right, boy," he says, his grip tightening on the bat. "All right. You asked for it."

He swings the bat into the side of the window. The wood splinters, loud as a gunshot. I scream at the sudden crack, and then the bat is raking along the frame, clearing away the last shards of glass still sticking to it. Roy's fingers grip either side of the frame like spider legs as he catapults himself through the open window. My eyes dart across the room, looking for something—*anything*—we can use to protect ourselves, but then Beckett is grabbing my hand, pulling me out of the back door and into the pines.

I put the phone to my ear.

"This is Evelyn Waverley," I shout to be heard over the low howl of a snow-drenched wind. "We're at the Campbell Christmas tree lot and someone is chasing us with a baseball bat—"

Three clicks and then the line goes dead. I've lost the signal.

"No, no, *no!*"

I hit the redial button, but it doesn't go through, and I have no idea if the operator heard a word I said. I slow down, trying to find a signal.

"Evelyn!" Beckett yells.

Roy is only a couple rows behind us, moving quicker than I would have thought possible. I put the phone back in my pocket and force my legs to go faster. Beckett doesn't let go of my hand as he weaves through row after row, into the deeper sections, where the trees are so dense, they're almost impossible to move through.

"Who—is—that?" I ask him, my breath coming out in short, cloudy gasps.

Beckett's jaw clenches. "My stepfather."

"You can run, boy, but you can't hide," Roy shouts into the night. And that's when it hits me.

We're running through snow.

"*Beckett,*" I gasp, pointing at our footsteps.

He curses. "We need something to hide them."

He pulls me even faster down another row, trying to put

more distance between us and his stepfather before turning to the tree closest to us and grabbing hold of a branch, leaning on it to break it off from the trunk.

"Where's a saw when you need one?" Beckett murmurs through his teeth.

Roy's footsteps are closer now, boots punching hard through packed snow. "Come out, come out, wherever you are."

My heart is beating so hard I swear it's going to punch right through my chest. I get on the other side of the branch and put my weight on it too.

"Please, God, please," I murmur.

Beckett jumps onto the branch. I do the same.

It starts to crack. "Please, please, *please*—"

We jump one more time. The branch snaps off.

"Come on," Beckett says, grabbing it and pushing me ahead of him. He drags the curtain of evergreen needles behind us, wiping away our footprints. But stopping took too much time, and we're moving slower with the branch.

Roy can't be more than three rows behind us now.

"Turn right," Beckett whispers, and I do as he says, starting down the row lengthwise. He drags the branch behind us, then clicks his tongue. I glance back. He jerks his head, signaling for me to crawl underneath one of the giant trees like we did the night of the party. I slide underneath. Beckett scuttles in right behind me, using the branch to smooth the area of snow we disrupted before pulling it beneath the tree and shielding us with it.

Roy stumbles onto the path.

"I know you're out here," he calls in an awful, singsong voice. I close my eyes and grit my teeth, willing myself not to scream. He starts toward us. My heart hammers so hard against my ribs I'm sure he can hear it, sure he's going to find us any second, sure he's going to pull us out from underneath this tree one right after the other.

The snow seeps into my jeans. My teeth chatter. The noise feels deafening.

*Please, no.*

Beckett rolls on top of me, pushing the edges of his coat down around my body, trying to keep me warm. He takes both of my mittened hands in his bare ones and presses his lips to my ear. I try to focus on his weight, on his warmth. Try to imagine I'm anywhere but here.

"No matter what happens," he whispers, his hands tightening around mine, "I won't let him hurt you."

Roy's footsteps crunch the snow in front of our tree. My eyes lock on the heel-toe motion of his boots as he walks by, listening for us.

My heart ratchets into my throat.

Roy stops.

I hold my breath.

Roy cocks his head, a wild look in his eyes, then starts walking again. Beckett waits for him to disappear down another row before murmuring, "We just have to wait for him to get far enough away, then we can circle back, get in your car, and head for the sheriff's office."

I nod. It sounds like a good plan. Sensible. I tell myself to focus on that, on the good, sensible plan that won't backfire, because Beckett's stepfather is drunk and slow and we are fast and clear-minded. This is going to be fine. We're going to be fine. *Everything* is going to be fine—

Roy turns down another path, moving steadily away from us.

I exhale.

"Two more rows," Beckett's voice rumbles against my ear. "Give him two more rows. That should give us enough room to maneuver without him catching up. Are you okay to keep running?"

"Yes," I whisper back.

"I'm sorry," he says, his voice breaking on the words.

I open my mouth, not even sure what I should say, but knowing I have to tell him that none of this is his fault, and he doesn't have to apologize because we're going to be fine, and—

The rising, tinkling notes of my phone ringing climb and fall through the air like an audible flare gun.

"Go!" Beckett shouts, pushing me out from under the tree just as Roy reappears on the path. Beckett scrambles out behind me, but his jacket catches on a branch. I reach down to help him get it off, my fingers fumbling over the fabric.

The baseball bat crashes into a branch over my head. I scream and stumble back.

Beckett jolts out of his jacket. He stands, facing Roy, his fists on either side of his face. "I don't want to fight you, Roy."

"Are you kiddin'?" Roy scoffs. "That's all you've ever wanted to do."

The baseball bat whips through the air as Roy swings it directly at Beckett's chest. Beckett jumps back, the tip of the bat whistling across the edge of his clothes.

"Evelyn, run!" Beckett yells.

The bat comes swinging down again, but Beckett is looking at me—he doesn't see it coming. I scramble forward, pulling him down by his knees just as the bat narrowly misses his head.

Roy grabs a fistful of my hair and tugs me back. Pain like a branding iron sears across my scalp. I claw at his wrists, desperately trying to grab hold, but my mittens slip down the leather cuffs of his jacket. Stars burst in my eyes as the pain intensifies, and suddenly I'm so disoriented, I can't do anything but scream.

Beckett's fist comes from out of nowhere, connecting hard across his stepfather's jaw. Roy lets go of me and stumbles back, dropping the bat. It goes sliding across the snow, ten feet away from us. I fold into the fetal position, gripping my head. Seconds pass but it feels like minutes, and then the sear of the branding iron softens to a dull throb. The stars scatter. My vision returns, and I suddenly realize I'm lying directly in between Beckett and Roy.

"You lay a hand on her again, and I swear to God, I'll kill you," Beckett tells him.

Roy puts his palm against the underside of his chin, cracking his neck. "I'd like to see you try."

Beckett swings at him again, punching Roy in the stomach, but Roy absorbs it, connecting his fist across Beckett's cheek.

I crawl toward the bat, praying Roy won't notice.

He does.

He turns toward me, screaming profanities, but Beckett is already there, punching him across the face again. Once. Twice. Three times. Roy staggers, then barrels into Beckett like a bull, flattening Beckett against the snow. He puts his hands around Beckett's throat and squeezes.

I scramble for the bat.

"Do you know your mom wishes you were never born?" Roy shouts into the starless night. "You were the one who dragged her down, needing shit all the time that she couldn't afford. *You're* the reason she has such a terrible life." He laughs as Beckett chokes. "Looks like she'll get her wish now."

My fingers curl around the wooden neck of the bat. I push myself up, the tip of the bat scraping against hard-packed snow.

"Roy!" I shout.

He looks up a millisecond before I swing.

The bat connects with his cheek. A sickening *CRACK!* echoes through the trees. Roy's body twists in an awful way as he falls over.

For a moment, I think I might have killed him, and not a single piece of me cares.

"Is he dead?" I ask in a vague, distant sort of way.

Beckett crouches next to him, searching for a pulse. "No. He's alive."

I grit my teeth.

"Is your phone still working?" Beckett asks. "We can call the sheriff back, ask them to send an ambulance."

I nod, even though a terrible part of me wants to leave Roy out here and let the cold finish him. I push that terrible impulse away as I reach for my phone and hold it out to Beckett. "Here—"

Roy's fingers snap out, pulling the bat from my hand.

A scream erupts from my throat.

"Go!" Beckett shouts, pushing himself up.

I turn and sprint ahead of him, toward the gift shop. Beckett stays directly behind me, keeping a hand on my spine as we run, even though I'm sure he could dart ahead of me, but he wants to keep me in front of him, wants to keep me safe.

I chance a look back.

Roy is following us, but he's slower now, stumbling into every tree.

We're going to make it.

My phone rings again.

I hold it up to my ear. "Hello?"

"This is the Christmas, Virginia police department," the voice of the operator speaks into the phone. "Sheriff Gates is at the scene. Where are you?"

I spot the blinking red-and-blue lights of the sheriff's cruiser through the trees. "We're almost to the parking lot."

"Okay, keep going," she tells me in a calm voice. "Where is the man that's chasing you?"

I glance back. "In the trees. Two rows behind us."

"You're going to be all right. Just keep run—"

A shot cracks through the air.

Roy's pulled a gun out of his pocket.

And it's aimed directly at Beckett.

# 29

## Beckett

***

The second bullet whizzes past my ear as we stumble into the lot.

The sheriff's car is twenty paces away from us. I push Evelyn toward it. "Go!"

She glances back at me as she runs, her eyes widening.

"I'm not going anywhere without you," she yells back at me, but she's already halfway to the sheriff, and then he's there, darting around his car, pulling her back. She tries to fight him off, to get back to me, but she's weak from running, and the sheriff tugs her safely behind the open driver's side door.

Relief floods my chest. Bill and Bee are shielded by their car too, although I don't know how they could have gotten here so quickly, and even though I want to run to them, I know if I move, Roy will fire his gun again, and I'm not willing to take the risk of him hitting any of the people I love.

"Beckett," Bill shouts. "Get over here!"

I shake my head at him as the sheriff pulls out his own gun, propping it above his open car door.

Everything slows as I turn to face Roy. The wind howling through the branches. The drumming of my heartbeat against my chest. The police lights gleaming across the gun's barrel in flashes of red and blue. The smile pulling at Roy's lips, slow and methodical, reminding me, grotesquely, of the Cheshire Cat.

Until he sees the sheriff.

Then his smile falters.

"It doesn't have to end like this Roy," I tell him, my voice strong despite the fear and adrenaline coursing through my body.

Roy shrugs. "Seems I'm already going to jail. What do I have to lose?"

"Everything, Roy," I tell him. "Everything."

For the first time, he looks...scared.

And even though my stepfather is the one with the gun, all I see when I look at him is a weak, pathetic kid who lost his soul to alcohol a long time ago. I know how easy it is to walk that path, the one where your heart becomes so bitter and your vision so clouded that all you see is a twisted version of reality. And in that moment, I see myself, what I could someday be if I choose to walk that same path. If I choose to keep isolating myself, to believe the worst about everybody, to let the pain of my past erase the joy of my future. I wonder, in a distant sort of way, if Roy didn't have people around to comfort him, to point him back to the truth, to the light, like I do. And I feel sorry for him. For all that he could have been, if only he'd chosen something different.

"You fire one more bullet, and I swear on all that is holy I'll put twenty in you," the sheriff calls out. He should have a clear shot, although I don't dare take my eyes off of Roy to check.

Roy grits his teeth, swaying back and forth on unsteady feet. A line of blood trickles from the cut on his cheek.

He raises his hands. Silver moonlight flashes across metal.

And then the gun drops into the snow.

My brain tries to process it all—the sheriff running for my stepfather, forcing him to his knees, cuffing his hands behind his back; Bill putting his arms around me, leading me back to the sheriff's cruiser; Evelyn and Bee embracing us both, everyone sobbing into my jacket as my entire body begins to shake.

"How did you know what was going on?" I ask Bill when he and Aunt Bee finally break apart from me. Evelyn starts to step away from me too, giving me room to breathe, but I wrap my arm around her and pull her back into my side.

I'm never letting her go again.

"My buddy Duke saw Roy drinking at a bar in the next town over. Said he was mumbling about the lot and looking like trouble as he left, so he gave me a call. Bee and I left enough money on the table to cover our check and ran to the car."

Sheriff Gates leads Roy to the cruiser. Roy gives me one last unreadable look as the sheriff puts his hand on his head and guides him into the backseat. Bee puts her arm around me again, and Bill stares Roy down until the sheriff's car pulls away.

The other police officers begin to mark out the scene, laying little yellow triangles with numbers on them on the broken window, by the gun, next to our footprints in the snow. An officer tells us he's just getting some things in order, and then he'll need to speak to each one of us individually to get our accounts of what happened. Bill invites him back to the farmhouse for coffee.

Through the swirling red-and-blue lights, I notice the

ring on Aunt Bee's left hand.

And despite everything that has just happened, I smile.

"I'm sorry you didn't get to finish your dinner," I tell them as we head back to the farmhouse ahead of the officer, Evelyn still tucked into my side.

Bee shakes her head. "Are you kidding? We were terrified when Bill got that call from Duke. I hate that we weren't here in time. We should've never gone out, not after he'd just visited."

"We thought he was on his way home," I remind her. "And I'm glad you weren't here. Who knows what Roy would have done?" I picture him pulling the gun out sooner, pointing it at Bill and Bee, using them to coerce me into his car.

"Are you okay?" I ask Evelyn as Bill and Bee walk ahead of us, Bill holding onto Bee's arm as he guides her over the icy patches.

Evelyn pushes me hard in the chest. "Don't you *ever* do anything like that to me again, Beckett Hawthorne, do you understand?"

My eyes narrow. "I couldn't take the chance of him hurting you."

"And what? You think I would've been just fine with him hurting *you*?" She places her hands on her hips and glares at me. "If we're going to make this work, we do *everything* together, including facing down madmen with guns. You jump, I jump, Jack."

My lips curve into a half-smirk. "Are you really quoting *Titanic* to me right now?"

She crosses her arms. "I'm serious. We face everything life throws at us together or not at all. Got it?"

"If you're a bird, I'm a bird."

"That's *The Notebook*."

"Felt right."

She narrows her eyes. "I don't believe you."

"I swear. We do everything together from here on out." I hold my arms out to her. "Now come here."

She shakes her head, but then she's sliding into them and resting her cheek against my chest. "I've never been so scared in my life."

"I told you I wasn't going to let him hurt you."

She rolls her eyes like I couldn't be a bigger idiot if I tried. "Not for me. For you." She glances up at me, tears rolling down her cheeks. "I can't lose you. Not when we've only just found each other."

I take her face in my hands and press my lips to her brow. She closes her eyes.

"Evelyn Waverley," I whisper, her name a sacred breath on my lips, "I can't promise you that I won't want to spend every single second of my life protecting you, or that I won't ever choose your safety over my own again, because that's all I want to do. Every day of my life, I want to choose you. But I think that's the point. If we choose each other, neither one of us will get left behind." I breathe in the scent of her hair. Apricots and honey. "Besides, I should be lecturing you about the same thing. What were you thinking, taking on Roy all by yourself?"

"I wasn't thinking," she says. "All I knew was that I couldn't let him hurt you."

"I felt the same way."

She narrows her eyes at me. "Fine. You're off the hook. *For now.*"

I wrap her up in my arms and thank God she's still here. Still with me.

We head inside and help Bee make coffee for the officers and for Evelyn's parents, who show up at the door looking panic stricken and frantic—the sheriff must have called them as we were leaving the lot. They wrap Evelyn in their arms and glare daggers at me, and I'm certain there's not a bone in either one of their bodies that wants me to date their daughter now, but Bill's hand on my shoulder is a source of comfort, a steady presence communicating his trust in me, and, somehow, I know everything's going to be all right.

The officer wants to interview us individually, but all it takes is a smile from Aunt Bee and a plate of Christmas cookies on the table for him to agree to let us all sit together, replaying everything that happened as he writes down our testimonies.

Evelyn and I sit on the same side of the table, and even though her parents are right next to her, her hand never leaves mine. I glance around the room, trying to push Roy's words out of my mind— *Do you know your mom wishes you were never born?*—because sitting here, in between the aunt and uncle who gave me a second chance, and the girl who actually made me want to take it, I know I'm right where I belong.

### ✳✳✳

Mom calls the next morning, sobbing after hearing about what Roy did.

"Baby, I'm so sorry." She says it over and over again, and I can hear the guilt, the anguish, the regret saturating her voice. "I should have left him a long time ago. I should have gotten clean a long time ago, and I know I haven't given you a single reason to believe me, but I promise you, this time will be different."

She tells me a local pastor has been dropping off food for her at her door.

"He's not one of those pushy ones," she says. "You know, the ones that make you feel like they're trying to sell you something? It feels like he actually cares about what happens to me."

He's been talking to her about the meaning of Christmas. About righting past wrongs. About new life. About hope.

"He makes me want to be a better person," she whispers, and it doesn't just sound like lip-service this time. It sounds like a promise.

After we hang up the phone, Mom calls Serena and confesses everything, telling her she was the one holding the heroin, not me—something I think Serena suspected all along. Mom asks her what she needs to do to make it right.

Serena begins the process of setting it all in motion, and while there's still a lot of paperwork to be done, by the end of the day, she calls and tells me that I'm a free man. I'm no longer required to fulfill any community service hours, and my criminal record has been expunged.

"Still planning on hitting the road when you turn eighteen and ruining your life?" Serena asks.

"Nah," I tell her. "I think I'll stay around here for a while. Apply for some scholarships. Did I tell you I'm playing violin again?"

"No, but I'm happy to hear it." Her chair squeaks, and I picture her there in her office, her ankles crossed on the corner of her desk. "Does that girl have anything to do with it? The one who was giving you all that trouble a few weeks ago?"

"She has everything to do with it."

"Sounds like you need to keep that one around."

"Believe me," I say, staring through the kitchen window at the snow-covered fields and the heavy gray clouds hanging low enough to brush the distant ice-covered trees. At the land that, when I first arrived, felt like just another stop on the collapsing one-way track that was my life, but that now feels, incomprehensibly, like home. "I'm planning on it."

***

I've never seen my uncle Bill cry. The closest I got was that night that he and Bee stood at the top of the basement steps, but he cries when I tell him I won't have a criminal record anymore, silent tears that slick his cheeks. He wraps me up in a bear hug.

"You always have a place here, son."

I lean into his warmth, and my own tears come hot and fast. I try to blink them away, but it's no use. That's how Aunt Bee finds us when she brings dinner over, carry-out from the same restaurant she and Bill had been at the night before—both of us holding each other and crying.

"I thought the three of us could finish that fancy dinner Bill and I started," she says, placing the brown paper bag in the center of the table. "There's steak and potatoes in there for everyone. Salad too, if I can get either one of you to eat it."

"I'll take mine upstairs," I tell her. "Let you two finish what you started last night."

Bee arches a brow. "You most certainly will not. You're as much a part of this family as anyone else, and besides"— she glances at Bill, a sudden blush tingeing her cheeks— "we have something to tell you. How do you feel about Bill and me getting married on Christmas Eve?"

"*This* Christmas Eve?"

Bee nods. "Lorna Riddle says she can throw it together with her daughter, Isla, even though it's only a couple weeks away."

"We don't need anything fancy," Bill insists. "But we're both too busy to plan it ourselves."

"And it's only going to be a handful of people anyway," Bee adds. "Ten, at the most, including our wedding co-ordinators."

Bill laughs and shakes his head. "You're delusional if you think the whole town won't turn up for it."

"It's true." I break open a roll, still warm from the oven, and spread butter across the middle. "They love you too much to let you get away with a small wedding."

She sighs. "Fine, we can have a party in the school gym afterward, *if* enough people RSVP. It will be Christmas Eve, you know. People do have lives."

"They'll RSVP," Bill says, taking a sip of the wine Bee poured for him.

My eyes dart back and forth between them, soaking in their warmth. "It's nice to see you both so happy."

Bill takes Bee's hand. "Kid, you have no idea."

"Actually, Bill, I think he does."

Evelyn calls me after dinner. I was shocked when her parents let her drive me to and from school today. I thought for sure they were never going to let her see me again.

"They can't hate you for something you had no control over, Beckett," she told me that morning as her Volkswagen glided over the salt-crusted interstate, the sun just beginning to peek over the horizon. "They actually said they really admire you for everything you've overcome, and that they owe you my life." She glanced over at me. "I'm pretty sure you could ask them for anything, and they'd give it you."

"There's only one thing I want, Evelyn Waverley."

She arched a brow. "And what is that?"

"You." I imagined the future spreading out before us, full of possibilities and challenges we would tackle together. "Just you."

There are patterns to be unlearned, issues I know I have to deal with, and a relationship with my mother that needs to be restored, but as the sun rose higher on the horizon and Evelyn pulled into town, I felt the physical turning of a page, and all I could think about was how thankful I was that Evelyn was there, a steady light guiding my ship through the darkness.

Bringing me home.

# Epilogue

## Evelyn

### * * *

"**I** cannot fix on the hour, or the spot, or the look, or the words, which laid the foundation. It is too long ago. I was in the middle before I knew that I had begun."

Beckett was a phenomenal Darcy. All of the local newspapers raved about him—*The Christmas Herald, The Williamsburg Gazette*—and even a few bigger ones, Boston and Chicago and Seattle, which picked up the story after seeing so many people like and comment on social media posts about it.

I attach the articles to every Ivy League application. Before Beckett, I would've been happy getting into any of them, but I'm really banking on Harvard or Columbia now that Beckett is Zooming with his old violin teacher in San Antonio again, who has some friends on the admissions boards at Juilliard in New York City and the New England Conservatory of Music in Boston. Beckett has begun taking lessons again, and even though he swears he's rusty and needs a lot of practice, all I hear when he plays are the purest, most soul-wrenching sounds I've ever heard in my life. He pours all of who he is—every particle, every hurt, every haunted memory—into his music, and no program can teach that. I do tease him that maybe he should go into acting after his stellar performance, which the *Herald* proclaimed "magnificent", and the *Gazette* called, "Brilliant! The *perfect* Darcy!" But he says Darcy is the only role he could ever play because all he had to do was be himself and talk to me instead of Elizabeth.

"If it were anyone else on that stage with me, I would've been terrible," he said as he held me in his arms on Uncle Bill and Aunt Bee's couch after our final performance, our sock feet intertwined, mugs of hot cocoa on our laps and the Keira Knightley version of *Pride and Prejudice* on the TV.

Now, Isla, Savannah, and I are helping Bee in the bride's room at First Presbyterian, placing her hat on her perfectly curled, snow-white hair and layering the short veil dotted with snowflake crystals across her face. She's wearing a simple ivory dress that skims just below her knees, and there's a matching jacket hanging on the door that Isla is gently doing some last-minute steaming on. Savannah, who got roped into taking on the odd wedding job for Riddle Bridal—provided she didn't have to actually *talk* to any of the brides about true love and happily-ever-afters—hands Bee her bouquet of white roses, snowdrops, and hydrangeas. The theme of the wedding, even though Bee insisted they didn't need one, is winter wonderland, and Isla and her mother have decorated the church with delicate birch branches lining the aisle and candles on every windowsill, each one ringed by white flowers laid to look like snow. Even Savannah choked up when we finished putting it all together.

She surprises me now by going against her own rule and talking to the bride. "Aunt Bee," she says, hesitantly. "Why did you decide to remarry Bill after all of this time?"

Bee thinks for a moment.

"Bill and I"—she exhales—"we were not the people we needed to be when we first married. We made mistakes. We hurt each other. But I think a part of us always knew we were meant to be together. It just took some growing apart for us to grow back together." She rolls her eyes, laughing at herself. "I only wish it hadn't taken fifty years, but then again, everything good happens in its own time. Rushing it never does anyone any good, but neither does putting off the real thing when it comes your way." Her eyes sparkle as she meets my gaze.

I smile and grasp the heart-shaped locket Beckett gave me on opening night. In it is a picture of Jane Austen on one side and an illustration of Darcy on the other. I looked up at him and asked, "Not a picture of you?"

"Not yet," he replied as he took it from my hands and clasped it around my neck. "I'm going to make it my goal to earn that spot over your heart. Darcy is just a place-holder until I do."

I always thought controlling every little thing would ensure my life would turn out exactly the way I wanted it to, but the beauty of life is that it surprises you, and I wouldn't trade the surprise of Beckett for anything in the world.

Beckett is my good thing. I didn't plan on him coming into my life this early—in truth, if I'd had the choice, I wouldn't have met anyone until I was well on my way to becoming the woman I've always dreamed of becoming, but Beckett has made it clear that his greatest desire is to help me get there, not keep me from it. We're going to learn the lesson Bill and Bee are imparting to us—we're going to help each other become the people we're meant to be. Grow together. Live and love and laugh and play and be our own little family, the two of us, inside of the larger family surrounding us—my parents and Aunt Allison, Uncle Bill and Aunt Bee. Because if I've learned anything from Jane Austen, it's that real love, whether in a romance, or in family, or in friendships, doesn't ask you to give up who you are, or keep you from becoming who you're meant to be—it comes alongside you. Supports you. Abides with you.

And just as much as Beckett wants to support my dreams, I want to support his. I don't want to have to lose him to find him again. When we make the choice to be together, I want it to be forever.

Bee gasps as she steps into the sanctuary and Beckett begins playing her down the aisle, low romantic notes thrumming over the strings of his violin. The whole town has shown up, just as Beckett predicted they would. The school gym is still decorated from the winter formal, where there will be food and music and dancing long into the night. Bill stands at the altar, rubbing tears from his cheeks as Bee makes her way toward him, a smile on her lips and love in her eyes.

I take a seat in the third row between my parents and Aunt Allison, who made it in for the play's opening night.

Beckett winks at me.

"He plays beautifully," Mom whispers to me.

Allison elbows me. "Turns out Darcy really is just a misunderstood soul."

Beckett continues staring at me through the service, the love in his eyes making my heart melt.

"Careful with that one," Allison tells me. "I don't think he's ever going to let you go."

"That's okay," I reply. "I don't want him to."

I rub the locket again, my thumb gliding over the inscription on the back, a paraphrased quote from Darcy—*I ardently admire and love you*—and smile back at him.

This Elizabeth has found her Mr. Darcy.

And she's never letting him go.

## A Look At:
## All I Want For Christmas is The Boy I Can't Have

What happens when you take a chance on someone unexpected?

Isla Riddle has been obsessed with True Love for as long as she can remember. Books, TV, movies—if it's a story about star-crossed lovers, ill-fated love, or love conquering all, Isla has read it, seen it, and talked nonstop about it. She's also dedicated her life to it by helping her mom build up Riddle's Bridal Boutique and Wedding Planning, a business they started together after her dad left town ... and they've just received their biggest break yet: a high society bride with a million-dollar budget.

August Harker doesn't have to think much about his life—it's already been planned for him. He has the parent-approved heiress girlfriend, the 4.0 GPA at an elite college preparatory school, and over a dozen lacrosse and debate team trophies. He has no reason to think his life won't turn out just like his dad's, which is exactly why he isn't into planning weddings, parties, or any other event where hundreds of his father's closest clients and legal associates discuss affidavits, jurisprudence, and all the things that make his father the most sought-after criminal defense attorney along the Eastern seaboard. It only reminds August that he'll be discussing the same things with the same people in ten years' time between glasses of champagne and unfortunate run-ins with the electric slide. However, planning a wedding is exactly where he finds himself as his older sister prepares to walk down the aisle.

As Isla works with August behind-the-scenes, she becomes more and more convinced that he's the one: the soulmate she's been waiting for. August feels it, too, that rightness of being with Isla, and as August hears Isla talk about dreams like they're real possessions that can be achieved, he dares to hope for another future entirely, one in which he can become what he's always wanted to be.

But can their love—and August's newly-resurrected dreams—survive the layers of expectations and ambitions that have been placed upon him?

*AVAILABLE DECEMBER 2021*

# Acknowledgements

### ✳✳✳

To God, first and foremost. Thank You for seeing me through the writing of this book and for Your constant love and care. You are my firm foundation, my stronghold, my everything. I could not do a second of this life without You.

To Rachel Del Grosso, and the entire Wise Wolf team. I am still in awe of how brilliantly and seamlessly you work, of the gorgeous covers, of the ingenious copyedits, and of the vision you are cultivating for the future of publishing. I am beyond grateful to be a part of this team.

To my agent, Andrea Somberg, for always being there for me whatever I need, big or small. You provide the continuous support every author dreams about, and I could not be more thankful for you.

To my author friends, who provide brainstorming services, creative support, a listening ear, and unending encouragement—Nova McBee, Marlena Graves, Lori Goldstein, Natalie Mae, Lorie Langdon, Kerry Winfrey, Kristy Boyce, Erin A. Craig, Becky Dean,

Elizabeth Van Tassel and all of the Kidlitnet Authors. To say you're the best doesn't even begin to describe it.

To Kristen, Alli, Maria, Carrie, Regan, and Karri, for always throwing the most incredible book birthday celebrations and making me feel like the most loved writer in the entire world. And to Mandy, Mysti, Andrea, and Stephanie, for nearly three decades of friendship, love, support, and encouragement—I am so incredibly thankful for you all.

To my parents, for crafting homes where I always felt safe, loved, and cherished, and to Jane, for the countless ways you saw this project through to the end.

To Nathan, for being the inspiration behind every romantic moment I write, and to Emerson and Caleb, for pouring endless amounts of joy and beauty into my days. God blessed me beyond measure when He gave me the three of you to call home.

To Jane Austen, for Pride and Prejudice, and for paving the way for all female writers. What a gift your books continue to be to this world.

And to the readers—I pray you will always know your worth and never let anyone take it from you. Happiest of readings to you, my friends.

# About the Author

### ✳✳✳

Chelsea Bobulski is a graduate of The Ohio State University with a degree in history, although she spent more of her class time writing stories than she should probably admit. Autumn is her favorite time of the year, thanks to college football, falling leaves, cozy fireplaces, and the countdown to the most magical holiday of them all: Christmas. She is the author of *The Wood* (2017) and *Remember Me* (2019). She grew up in Columbus, Ohio, but now resides in northwest Ohio with her husband, two children, and one very emotive German Shepherd/Lab mix.